Can a Girl and a Boy be...
Just
Friends?

Sumrit Shahi, just twenty-four years old, is one of the youngest bestselling authors in the country.

He wrote his first novel, *Just Friends*, at the age of seventeen which became a bestseller, followed by another successful novel *Never Kiss Your Best Friend.*

Sumrit is also a screenwriter and has written for six youth-based shows including *Sadda Haq: My Life, My Choice* on Channel V India which won the Youth Show (Fiction) category at the Zee Gold Awards in 2014 and at the Indian Telly Awards in 2014 and 2015; *Million Dollar Girl: From Banaras to Paris* also on Channel V; *Boyz* on Big Magic Entertainment; *Twist Wala Love* and *Secret Diaries* on Channel V; *BIG F* on MTV India and *Ek Veer Ki Ardaas...Veera* on Star Plus to his credit.

In 2015, the author was chosen by *Hindustan Times* in the list of Top 30 Under 30 young achievers in the country, terming him as a 'writing rockstar of the young'. He is currently based in Chandigarh.

Can a Girl and a Boy be...

Just Friends?

SUMRIT SHAHI

RUPA

Published by
Rupa Publications India Pvt. Ltd 2017
7/16, Ansari Road, Daryaganj
New Delhi 110002

Sales centres:
Allahabad Bengaluru Chennai
Hyderabad Jaipur Kathmandu
Kolkata Mumbai

ISBN: 978-81-291-4837-7

First impression 2017

10 9 8 7 6 5 4 3 2 1

Indebted to,
His Holiness Satguru Baba Hardev Singh Ji Maharaj,
who taught me that God is formless (*Nirankar*).
Mrs Inderjeet Kohli (my grandmother)—your hands still rock
the cradle of my life...to sleep, to contentment.
Mrs Smiley Shahi (my mother)—you burned your necessities
to fulfil my desires.
Mr Sukhjit Shahi (my father)—for being my shadow,
indispensable yet flexible.

Ek tuhi Nirankar
Mein teri sharan han
Mainu baksh lo

Contents

A Word or Two

Teenage is the most confusing, challenging, adventurous yet insightful years in one's journey of life.

An age, when equations change before an eye blink, when everything that begins with 'L'...ends into lust...even if it is love. When friends become your breath and you their soul.

Come realize and relive these years... With the fable of two teenagers, as they sit at airport and share their tryst of Living, Liking, Lusting, Loving, Losing, Learning...all to unknowingly answer for each other the biggest question that haunts their lives, respectively and collectively.

'Can a girl and a boy be just friends?'

Sumrit Shahi
www.sumritshahi.weebly.com
sumrit.shahi@ssla.edu.in

1

Of Endings and Beginnings

Aaryan
THE PRESENT

Date: 7th April 2010
Time: Early Morning
Location: Hotel M, Singapore

> *Destiny conceals what dreams reveal.*
> *When darkness exudes warmth, you dream...*
> *She sits with me,*
> *laughter and tears—the two impressions of every expression,*
> *darkness again...*
> *She caresses my hair,*
> *silk soft—her fingers,*
> *warm, motherly—her lap, darkness again...*
> *Her heavy breath engulf me,*
> *darkness again...*
> *A high mountain, a floating cloud, a setting sun, a soaring*
> *bird—the zenith of 'our existence',*
> *darkness again...*

Light—it murders the darkness...the dream.

I got up with a start. It was the same dream again—*the dream which like a shadow accompanied me through the day, vague yet intense; the dream like a mirror, a ghost living through the night, haunting my existence.*

I sat up in my bed and reached for the bottle of water kept on the side table. My lips kissed the top of the bottle and the liquid trickled down my throat in its most pious form. Boza would have hated this. 'Use a glass,' she would have said angrily had she been here...only if she were here. I smiled in the warmth of my best friend's memory.

I got out of bed, walked up to the window and drew the curtains away. *Singapore.* My dream stared back at me; the dream I had lived for ever since I had met Ishita a year ago, back in India.

'I love her,' I had declared to Boza and all my other friends, soon after our three-day encounter had seeped into every crevice and every pore of my mind, my body and my heart.

The telephone rang and I rushed to pick up the call. 'Hello,' I said carefully.

'Aaryan, I just called to wake you up. Is everything packed?' asked Mom, her voice laced with concern.

'Yes Mom, everything done,' I replied and looked around to find my bag resting peacefully in the temporary darkness that could dissolve with one touch of the switch.

'Finally, my son is returning to India after a week. Dad is so proud of you; he has been boasting about your achievement to all and sundry.'

I smiled at myself—an achievement that was a façade; a false escape; a prelude to the harsh reality. I was basically a loser; a loser who had lost friendship and love, both.

'Aaryan! Aaryan!' Mom's repetition of my name brought

me back to the real mirage I considered life.

'Y...yes, Mom,' I replied.

'Son, all the best for your flight. We will see you at the airport.'

'Alright, Mom. Bye.'

And just as I was about to hang up, Mom began, 'By the way, I forgot to tell you...Karan had called last night. She is still in the ICU. We all are praying for her.'

Emotions choked my throat, leaving me with no alternative but to disconnect the call.

※

Aaryan
THE PAST

Date: 9 August 2009
Time: 1.30 p.m.
Location: India Habitat Centre,
           New Delhi

> *Strangers till yesterday,*
> *Acquaintances today,*
> *Friends now.*

A seventeen-year-old boy and a seventeen-year-old girl sat in an upscale restaurant at India Habitat Centre, New Delhi. The boy in question is me, Aaryan Gill. I am tall and admirably long and with her in front of me, hard too...Oops, my honourable, hormonal hopes!

The girl in front of me is Ishita. She is from Singapore and she is my dream, my destiny, for the past two days at least!

'So, what type of music do you like?' she asked, taking a

large sip from the cold coffee glass.

'Ummm…soft, subtle, sweet…seductive,' I replied saucily.

She stayed silent for a moment before saying, 'Hmmm…so Mr Aaryan, what soft, subtle, sweet and not to forget, seductive song would you like to dedicate to me, that is, if you had to?'

I grinned sheepishly when she fired the question at me as it totally caught me off guard. The way her hazel blue eyes stared at me I couldn't help but try deciphering the hidden romantic agenda the question carried, making it all the more difficult for me to answer. But something inside prodded me to be at my wittiest best, 'I don't know. It will probably be something unplugged, you know from my heart to your heart.'

'*1-1, the flirt game is on,*' I excitedly thought.

'So, when are you going back to Singapore?' I questioned after a few seconds on hearing nothing from her in reply.

'I think it'll be…*When you say nothing at all,*' she replied, as if addressing her own question and ignoring mine.

'*Oh yes, she did get the catch, Mr Wit-hit, 2-1.*' She was leading while I was happy being led.

'So what makes you smile or shall I say, blush?' she asked, looking straight into my eyes.

'*3-1. Go baby, you win at my expense.*'

'The fact that you so cleverly extracted your farewell treat from me…or is it that you won't get to see and talk to me after tomorrow?' she asked.

Pop! The bubble just burst by a pin named reality. She was going back tomorrow and we would probably never meet again.

'Excuse me, I'll be back in a jiffy,' she said as she looked in the direction of the washroom. 'Be ready with an answer that bowls me off,' she said, touching me momentarily on my shoulder. I couldn't help but mutter to myself as I saw her proceed, 'Girl, you sure did bowl me out.'

I was still dreaming; to be more precise, fantasizing, when she returned.

'Still thinking of an answer,' she commented as soon as she caught me in the thoughts.

'Err...ummm...no. It's just that you are going away tomorrow,' I replied lamely, trying to cover up for my bold thoughts.

'You already occupy a place in my virtual world, I mean, Facebook, MSN and all, silly,' she said in such a cute tone that the gloom engulfing my face suddenly broke into a glorious smile.

'And we have our whole life ahead. We are just seventeen and not to forget, Singapore is a nice country to holiday in,' I replied, sounding hopeful.

'I think we should finish this quickly. My teacher should be here, somewhere around,' she said, surprising me with her abrupt, discomforting tone.

Silently she kept looking down, unable to meet my eyes.

Aaryan
THE PRESENT

Date: 7 April 2010
Time: 9 a.m.
Location: A road leading to Changi Airport, Singapore

> *It's amazing*
> *How you can speak*
> *right to my heart.*
> *Without saying a word,*
> *you can light up the dark.*
> *Try as I may,*
> *I could never explain*

> *what I hear when*
> *you don't say a thing.*
> *You say it the best when you say nothing at all.*

Ronan Keating's voice echoed in the taxi, reminding me of that distant afternoon of almost a year ago. At that time I had never thought that a casual flirtation would trigger such emotions that would result in upsetting my calm and complacent world into a humongous metamorphosis. Nor could have anyone thought that I, an ordinary student, would end up here in Singapore, living my dream...but at a cost.

Five minutes before I reached the airport, the song ended. So this is what love and loss is all about, I thought. As the taxi came to a halt in the parking lot, I couldn't help the philosophical salt in my cerebral juice from deducing that my first and final journey had left an imprint on my life—a life where I had lived, liked, lusted, lost, learned and LOVED.

꠴

Aaryan
THE PAST

Date: 20 August 2009
Time: 10.30 p.m.
Location: Inside my dorm, B.N.
         World School, Gurgaon

> **And now you are gone.**
> *A moment ago you were here and now you are not.*
> *Was this destined to be: a preconceived plot,*
> *A farewell kiss and some unsaid words*
> *as you took flight, my migratory bird?*

'We will stay in touch,' you promised and I am sure
the day we hold hands again will I feel secure.
You acted brave and maintained your poise
and I had to be supportive, though did I have a choice?
Assurance is what my heart gets when left to ponder over
you up there.
I now know why they say
'distance makes the heart grow fonder.'

—*Aaryan*

※

Tanie
THE PRESENT

Date: 7 April 2010
Time: 9 a.m.
Location: Inside a bookshop at
            Changi Airport

'On which side are the romance fiction kept?' I inquired, as the middle-aged Indian owner of the book shop shot at me a totally accustomed, so-this-small-little-girl-wants-romance, the all-knowing look!

The overwhelming urge to thrust my passport into his face subsided as he quickly moved out of focus. 'This way,' he muttered mechanically.

So what if I owned a petite frame and stood at five feet two inches (God bless Chanel, for the high heels!) Even if it seemed that I still read Sydney Sheldon secretly in claustrophobic closets or under my blanket could not suppress the happiness I brimmed with at the moment.

For all of sixteen, I had travelled to Singapore all by myself, registered a win in the Model United Nations conference, found the new shade of the Mac nail-paint I had been searching for eternity, not lost any money, received the offer of a drink from a real cute Australian guy at the MUN and most importantly, managed to live off and away from the memory of the night before I landed here—the memory which I had feared would bubble up with every passing nanosecond.

'So, is there a particular favourite or is it a new genre for you?' queried the sadist, observing my vacant, dreamy look.

Ignoring his question, I started to scan through the shelves. After a detailed review, I finally chose this rather cute looking book, *A Walk to Remember* by Nicholas Sparks. This was the perfect way to distract me from the five-foot-eleven-inch, average-built, curly-black-haired guy with the most intense set of eyes and a goofy, flirtatious smile playing on the corners of his lips, there stood, sat or perhaps lay waiting for me. I had to answer Sumer and there was no escape.

I proceeded towards the cash counter. '23.50 dollars,' announced the cashier.

As I searched through my jeans pocket, which was full of specimens ranging from empty chewing gum wrappers to tissue papers from Burger King, I victoriously giggled at my unnoticed defiance of keeping chewing gum in a country known for its ban. As I dug in further to procure the cash, my hands brushed upon the familiar crumpled piece of paper.

'Read this once you are in Singapore,' Sumer had written on this small, unevenly torn note the night before I left for Singapore. I had felt strange—acting strangely with the best friend who wasn't entitled to the adjective 'best' any longer.

'23.50 dollars, madam,' murmured the cashier rather loudly.

'What was that?' I questioned earnestly, recovering from my stupor. She shot me a smile—a forced, constrained smile;

a smile sugared with the sour explicit message it hid.

'Madam, the book; do you want it or not?'

'Huh? Obviously...here,' said I, quickly handing over the money and realizing what the loud announcement was meant to convey and how my supposedly best friend was again occupying my mind more than the religiously shopped clothes, the new Armani fragrance I had feverishly bargained for in the China market and the many small knick-knacks that rested peacefully before they were to be exhibited to friends and foes galore.

'And now I know why love sells,' I gauged the feeble sarcasm in the cashier's voice as it trailed off, with me walking out of the store towards the boarding area.

'All passengers travelling with Air India scheduled for New Delhi, India, at 13.00 hours, are requested to heed with a technical problem in the engine. Therefore the takeoff time is postponed by an hour.'

'How convenient,' I said in exasperation.

'Inconvenience is regretted,' the melancholic melody ended, as if mocking my last sentence.

I parked my ass on a comfortable sofa in the boarding lounge. With all my luggage checked in and my handbag serving me as a footrest, feeling at home more than ever before, I decided to check the crowd out for the cute guys, or ugly aunties, or the cuddly babies—out of whom one would be sharing my armrest for the next seven hours. Amidst all this randomness, I still couldn't help but think of Sumer. 'Tanie, your relaxation makes me uncomfortable yaar. Just sit, okay?' he would have said if he were here.

'Stop! Stop! Stop!' I took a deep breath and ordered myself loudly, forgetting that I sat in the midst of a crowd. Dodging some obvious stares, I ducked my head into the book I had just bought, using it as a shield.

'Such a lovely book can definitely be used for better purposes, like reading for instance.' Closing the book shut, I looked up at the master of the voice who had walked up to me.

'Excuse me?'

'I am sure there's more to this book than using it to hide your face after enacting a sweet satire on Ramdev,' he added. I couldn't help but laugh.

'I'm Aaryan,' he said, extending his hand.

'Hi,' I gave a verbal embrace. He withdrew his hand.

'So what brings you here?' he questioned politely.

Does he want to know if I am travelling alone? I thought. I should have listened to Mom and carried the pepper spray.

'Uh...I will, then...see you around,' said he, sensing my obvious nervousness and turning around to leave.

'Ummm...I came here for an MUN. I mean...'

'A Model United Nations conference,' he completed the explanation, leaving me open mouthed.

I visualized the flabbergasted look I must have portrayed. 'Not many people know about the whole concept,' I said, justifying my stupefied expression.

'I know. I mean not many people know...I did an MUN myself last year.'

'You did?' He had got me interested.

'Yeah, may I?'

'It's a free country,' I joked and made room for him on the sofa. 'By the way, I am Tanie,' I introduced myself.

'Tanie, glad to meet a fellow MUNer,' he said, throwing a smile that radiated confidence. Sometimes strangers are sweet... he was cute looking, anyway.

'So, what brings you here?' it was my turn to know.

'My destiny and my dream,' he replied, adding, 'anyway, it's time I went back home to Chandigarh.'

'Chandigarh?' I asked, surprised.

'Yes, why?' he asked, taking off his frames.

'Which sector?' I questioned, revealing a smug smile.

'And they say it is a small, small world...I live in Sector 8,' he nonchalantly informed.

'I live in Sector 27,' I replied, wondering if God had deliberately sent a stranger-angel in my strange life. 'So you came here for studies?' I asked, realizing that the obvious questions were going to end soon.

'Yes...even that.' His reply surprised me.

'I didn't get you,' I said.

'Tanie, can I ask you something?' he questioned with a sudden seriousness.

'Umm...sure,' I answered. My curiosity had reached its peak.

'Why did you buy this book?' he fired an easy yet uncomfortable question.

'Maybe,' I began, choosing my words and reasons carefully 'maybe...I like love stories.'

'I see,' he said in a tone which clearly spoke of his dissatisfaction with the answer.

'And there are thoughts, which I want to forget till I reach back home,' I found myself blurting out the truth.

'You want some coffee?' he asked while his abstractness started to intrigue me.

'Sure...I'll come along.' Guys mixing sedatives in coffee was a näive but real thought that plagued me.

'Okay,' he said and we both got up to move towards the Starbucks counter.

'One iced mocha and one Espresso pleaseeeeee...' Aaryan sang out at the cash counter.

'23 dollars,' the cashier replied.

'I...I just got my currency exchanged into Indian rupees,'

Aaryan began embarrassedly. 'So, can you pay?'

So like Sumer, I thought. Ugh, I didn't have to think about him. Stop!

'Umm...I could go back and get some dollars, if you don't have any,' he suggested carefully, ending the awkward silence.

'No...it's okay. I was just thinking about someone...Here.' I fished in my jeans pocket to procure the leftover cash and scooped out everything that felt like paper (money) in haste, not realizing that in the action, Sumer's note would fall from my pocket.

⁂

'My coffee is no good,' I commented, taking a sip from the watery, cold coffee.

'It's best when served hot,' he replied, mixing some sugar in his coffee and words.

Did he just flirt with me? I wondered! I'll pretend I am a nerd and he will fly away. Simple, isn't it?

'So what did you study here, Aaryan?' I looked around, only to find him bending down. 'What happened?' I asked, as he stood up, smiling fishily. 'What?' I asked.

'Nothing,' he replied.

We walked back to our original seats.

'So Tanie, do you like stories?' Aaryan asked me once we were seated again.

'Hmmm...yeah, depends,' I replied innocently.

'Would you want to listen to a story which has teenage love, MUN, best friends, Singapore and Chandigarh too?' he asked.

'Seems interesting,' I replied, meaning every word.

'Yeah, may be...so, there's only one way to find out, I think,' he smiled.

And then, he began his story, knowing that he would get to hear one as well.

2

He Lives and Lusts...

Aaryan
THE PAST

Girl: 'Aaryan...'
Boy: 'Hmmm...?'
Girl: 'At least look at me; this is important!'
Boy: 'Okay...what?'
Girl: 'Here, take this tranquillizer first.'
Boy: 'Rhea, what?'
Girl: 'I am...so, do you love me?'
Boy: 'Love...I...you...yeah!'
Girl: 'Okay, then have this first. Yes, easy baby...just sit back and relax... Here, let me open it for you. Don't worry, it won't take much time. C'mon, now take it down...that's better. Have some more of it, you'll feel relaxed later, I guarantee. Here take some more water.'
(The boy gulps down the medicine, looking confused.)
Boy: 'Huh! What was that for?'
Girl: 'Aaryan...I missed it.'
Boy: 'Missed what?'

Girl (in a low voice): 'The period.'

Boy (casually): 'Oh, don't worry. Nobody would come to know.'

Girl (in tears): 'Oh, they will. Sooner or later, they will.'

Boy: 'They won't and even if they do, it's not as if they will kill you or anything. I have missed so many periods and got caught...the worst has been suspension.'

Girl (confused): 'You missing periods?'

Boy (confidently): 'Yeah.'

Girl: 'But you're a guy, you...you can't miss periods.'

Boy: 'Huh? Can't boys miss periods and enjoy...Should only girls have all the fun?'

Girl (angrily): 'Are you insane? I have missed my period here and you think it is a joke.'

Boy (calmly): 'There is nothing to get paranoid about. No more bunking for you, if you can't handle it.'

Girl: 'Bunking?'

Boy: 'Hey, wait a second, Rhea. Are you talking about the... period?'

Girl (frantically): 'Yes.'

Boy:...

I started laughing hysterically.

'Cut! Aaryan, we are almost through,' announced Batra, our supposed director, scriptwriter, producer in his best professional tone.

'Dude, how can I help it? The way Rhea said "yes", it almost sounded like she was happy about missing the periods.'

I cut him short before he could present his visionary justification.

'It's not funny, Aaryan,' intervened Batra. Panic! His emotional drive was in the fourth gear now.

'Then let's make it funny. How about this, when Rhea tells the that she has skipped it...I'd say, "That's great. I've spared you the pain." You see, it's a pun.'

My laughter echoed through the empty performance room where our little group had been trying to practise for our little skit on teenage pregnancy to be staged on the Student Awareness Day.

'Hun...hun...hun...' Batra's peculiarly squeaky violin-laughter signalled that all was fine. The brakes had been pressed at the right time. Phew! Safely parked!

'But the dialogues should be crisp and classy. Not so... hormonal,' said Chimmy, the rich yet intelligent, surprisingly hardworking and dedicated north-eastern girl by physical, chemical and biological combinations, chiming in from one corner.

'No, I think Aaryan is right. The skit should be funny and the dialogues should be more rooted, kind of earthy and grassy,' interrupted Boza, my Tibetan best friend, defending me.

Chimmy threw a cold look towards her.

Great North-East versus Tibet again...chopstick fight! 'Help us, Oh International Lord!' I smirked to myself.

'I heard someone mention grass(y),' groaned Karan, the pseudo from Singapore, stirring from his self-imposed slumber, from one corner of the room. If his life was to be written down on paper, his biography would have only three chapters—drinking, doping, doing everything which classified as good for nothing.

'Guys, please can we get back to work?' pleaded Batra, the sincere, small-town, scholarship holder; all in all, the misfit in our entire group.

'Guy? Me? I'm offended. I am staging a walkout,' announced Rhea in a theatrical manner, a terrible actor as she was. No one reacted to her attempt at satire. Ouch, a silent slap hurts the most!

'Okay, guys and Rhea, let's do this for the last time. Lunch begins soon,' I volunteered.

I should have been honoured with a bravery award for having an off-and on-screen girlfriend as intricately dumb as Rhea. She was like the prom queen minus the blonde hair, a model walk minus the long legs and a superstar minus the stardom.

'Just for you, baby,' she responded by throwing a kiss at me.

'I caught it... Oh it's salty,' said Karan with stony sarcasm.

'Ignore,' I signalled to her.

'Okay, let's start,' said Batra pleadingly and we duly complied with our theatre guru.

※

Five years ago my father had said, probably on getting inspired by *Kabhi Khushi Kabhie Gham*, 'Son, boarding school will make a man out of you.'

I was twelve then; puberty had begun to take its toll physically but mentally, I now deduce, I was a child. 'But, I don't want to go. See, I am growing a moustache,' I said, pointing towards the faint line of hair that outlined my lips. 'And now the Pizza Hut lady never says, "Yes, ma'am" when I ask for home delivery,' I said in my defence.

'Yes, big boy,' he laughed at my intentional innocence.

At that point of time, I had had a strong urge to show him my internet history, to tell him about the sprouting of the once-seeded plant into a long coconut tree. Yes, the nuts had grown too, but common sense took centre stage and I decided against telling him that I no longer believed in his answer of babies being secretly left on the roof when the parents prayed in different positions at night (what is more, once I had seen them 'praying'). Needless to say, I now knew it wasn't at all about praying; rather, it was all about playing.

So that is how I reached here from the quiet city of Chandigarh to the concrete jungle that Gurgaon is. The first time I set foot in B.N. World School, all myths and preconceived notions about the normal Indian hostel vanished into thin air as I surveyed the colossal 120 acres, which later, I would realize, would serve me more than just food, clothing and shelter.

Then I remembered the evening in the thirteenth year of my life, the dump yard near the abandoned basketball court where I had authentically learned from Marine, a French girl, how to execute the French kiss. These are memories which you cannot forget when you study in an international school.

'There is swimming, basketball, tennis, horse riding; there you can skate or learn to chip and putt.' This had been sung to us by the admissions coordinator, while I had checked out her butt. 'The dorms are air conditioned, the food multi-cuisine. He will get to study an international curriculum and stay (I had expected her to say 'sleep') with students from over twenty-five countries.'

Less studies and international buddies—I loved my parents for being so large and international hearted.

⁂

'Eighth period over,' boomed a mechanized voice out of the speakers, forcing me to bounce back into the present.

'Lunch,' Chimmy announced.

'What's for lunch today?' Karan asked.

'Rice and some Indian grass, I mean, some green veggie,' Boza whined.

'They are serving grass?' Karan loved to irritate us with his silly jokes. Grass is green, so is weed (Karan's grass).

'That was so funny, Karan,' Rhea stood there laughing, with

no hint of sarcasm but with an overdose of sincerity.

'Dude, your girl is funny. She laughs genuinely on every PJ,' Boza whispered in my ear.

'If you can't laugh with her, don't laugh at her,' I replied back, not meaning a single word (yup, that's me).

She laughed, I laughed, problem solved.

Boza Korbi, the Tibetan tweety, had been my best friend since the past three years.

Love for English—check.

Taste for non-vegetarian food—check.

Taste for the first Bacardi breezer together—check.

Worst example for each other—check.

Last year our friendship had run into rough weather, my love life was seething from a drought and hers was lost in a dry, long-distance desert.

We had kissed.

She was pissed.

No talk for two months—each other we missed.

And slowly spring came.

And then everything was the same.

I needed her, you see. I obviously still do. Anyone would, if the friend in question is 'activity in-charge' in a residential school. Courtesy her, we got the chance to go out (of campus) often. She was one of the popular poppies, befriending the useful guys and the ever-so usable girls.

❧

'Lunch begins,' we heard the same crass cacophony after ten minutes as we sat in the dining hall, inhaling the exotic aroma of the green matter which I suspect originated in the overgrowth near the kitchen door.

'It's surprising how grass isn't exciting me,' Karan casually commented and we all started to laugh.

'Aaryan, will you come with me to buy tuck?' Rhea suddenly questioned, exuding claustrophobic cuteness. The laughter subsided; spotlight shifted.

'Hmmm…okay, in the evening.'

It was Monday. Raju, the 'caring guard', would be on duty. I smiled mischievously, thinking of the prospective guilty indulgences that would accompany the evening.

'Ooh!' I groaned. Boza had kicked me under the table.

'What happened?' Rhea asked.

'Nothing,' I replied, eyeing Boza who was giving me the dog-I-know-you-are-fantasizing look.

❦

The next day in school, not in class (as usual).

'I have got some news,' I announced.

'Great. Type it out then,' Boza replied. We were in the editorial room working on the next issue of the school newspaper.

'Don't worry, everyone will soon know anyway,' I said.

'Know what?' she asked, shooting at me, a suspicious look.

'I broke up, again,' I answered casually.

'What? You broke up with Rhea?'

'Easy Booze, I have promised to stay friends,' I replied in earnest.

'Aaryan, you are incorrigible,' she sighed in exasperation.

'And guess what?' I continued.

'What?' she asked, looking up from the truckload of paperwork she was riding on.

'She literally left a mark on me,' I indicated towards the faintly visible yet fiercely painful nail-scratch under my left eye.

I laughed, she laughed, problem solved.

'She actually did this? But why, how, when?'

'Last evening. The tuck shop, remember?' I replied.

'No wonder she wasn't around for breakfast,' Boza analyzed.

'She's skipping school,' I filled in.

'Why?'

Before I could answer her, the door opened and I heard Karan shout out, 'Is it true about Rhea and you?'

'Yes,' I cut him short.

'So you did physically assault her?' he observed solemnly.

'Huh, what? Physical assault? She merely chipped a nail, damn it,' I protested.

'But I overheard her roommate talking to her friend in the academic block,' he offered in explanation.

'Looks like she nailed Aaryan on this one,' Boza's intelligent joke succeeded in extracting spontaneous laughter.

'All is fine unless she is admitted in the medical centre,' I predicted, after a little jaw flexing.

'What after that?' asked Karan.

Boza replied for me, 'It depends. There could be acquisitions. Bang!'

'You mean outright rape?' Karan looked concerned.

'Every bang is not chitty-chitty, bang-bang,' she mused and continued, 'anyway, it could begin with Aaryan's rough hands scaling her cherry cheeks, she pleading to let go and he saying no-na-na-no-no.' Boza didn't give us time to laugh again, 'With Aaryan asking her to help him with the whole job.'

'Really?' Karan's eyes grew bigger.

'If you could think with your brain for some time,' Boza suggested, before carrying on with her filmy interpretation. 'The poor little tulip. Actually, not so little; she is pretty tall, right?'

'Yes,' I answered, enjoying Karan's expressions led by Boza's impressions.

'So where was I? Yes, the poor little tulip—young, naive, freshly bloomed in the brightest shade of pink; cup shaped and I don't mean you-know-what, okay?' she said abruptly, knowing our testosterone-injected imaging capabilities.

We just smiled.

'The tulip stands alive, waiting to enjoy the sunlight, the air, the butterflies, the bees and guess what happens?' she asked, giving a dramatic pause.

'She gets sucked of her juice and then snapped and crumpled, her petals fall off and she is left naked. All she can see is a long, bare stick which is so thorny,' I offered, well aware of the hidden connotations.

'You are sick,' she said each word slowly.

The guys laughed, the girl laughed, problem solved.

Though at that point all of it sounded and seemed amusing, the undeniable reality was that once the rumour mills gathered momentum, my life would suffer from rough dry weather. Karan saw my smile falter. 'It won't reach the authorities; it never has,' suggested Karan.

Boza sighed, 'You want me to go and talk to her?'

She knew she would have to be involved sooner or later. 'Not needed,' I answered, supporting my head with my hands, with worry over the ideas it generated.

'Well, what did you cite as the reason for the break up?' Karan carefully asked me.

'Honestly, this time I tried being original. I mean the things won't work out, I have to study now, I don't want you and me to end up on a sigh, are all overused lines with underperformed results.'

'Then?' asked Boza this time.

'Well, I just told her I think my future isn't a straight road; it's a straight rod. I want to try the plains; the mountains don't work for me anymore...it's a transition,' I paused and grinned, looking at their shocked faces.

'The plan would have worked. I know she would be too embarrassed to tell everyone that her boyfriend was gay. For a "beauty queen" like her, her sensuality would be questioned by the masses and the classes. The clever calculation was almost there, had I not kissed her and hugged her tight enough, a few minutes ago. As our intensity grew, so did something down there. I should have known while my testosterone was on an all-time high, her estrogen had hit a rocky low. She must have felt let down,' I said, stressing the last line for Boza.

'Dude, you are a hitch, a sexy one,' Karan got up to hug me.

'Let me Google the local museum and tell them that we have a masterpiece here,' Boza announced, a grin breaking on her face a few seconds later.

The hi-five boys laughed; the museum-calling girl laughed; problem solved.

'Alright baby, miss me. I'm going for Pandey's tortuous trigonometry,' announced Karan in his best imitation of Rhea. 'You guys coming along?' he asked in his normal baritone.

If the break up was suicide, doing Maths soon afterwards meant homicide

'No,' I replied.

'We are,' Boza said.

'We are not going,' I said.

'We are,' Boza said.

'Okay, I am!' Karan shouted. 'Pandey will screw me otherwise. He saw me swiping Batra's entry pass.'

'He will screw you with his compass?' I loved it when Boza slurred over high-tech jokes.

'Whatever,' he said and left.

'Here, read this,' said Boza, handing me an article submitted by a Class X student for our school newspaper.

Students Charter

We, the students of B.N. World School, solemnly pledge to trouble technology, if it cannot be tamed. Play, dress up with it, trying to enter class, swiping your friend's special student's pass—scratch its back, swipe it in-n-out. It's just liberal experimenting after all. If caught in action, your reaction—the 'lost lamb' look; do anything to protect your identity. You are the selected one. The onus of the nation lies on you. Tell them how hazardous and disrespectful it is to sit in class for forty minutes. It is a block to the mental stock. Your right to expression entitles you to do graffiti in the school washrooms, refrain from cliched caricatures and multi-language abuses; think out of the box and you shall succeed. Don't consume vodka in class as it's difficult to arrange for peppermint later. Don't booze as the teacher will not let you snooze. Be practical; don't talk in class and keep the decibel volume low; everyone can SMS anyway. Don't hide your cell phone in your bag; the underclothes feel neglected. Don't listen to songs on your iPod during English; not every English song is improving the language. Try the vintage stuff though. Don't start snuggling up with your girl/boy during value education, saying, 'We are just practically showing everyone what love is.' Try to be naughty, but don't pinch the French teacher's ass. Don't use artificial fart bombs; natural ones can work wonders.

You are vested with laptops for study, fast-speed internet for research. Don't download porn on the headmaster's IP address; you can play clan counter-strike though.

'You have a new e-mail,' Boza's Apple beeped and I stopped reading the (im) moral, (im) mature article.

'Whose is it?' I asked.

'Finally,' she exclaimed 'the DPMUN 2008.'

'What?'

She ignored me. 'I am going to the activity coordinator's room; you stay here,' she ordered me and left. With nothing else to do, I logged on to Facebook on the Vice Principal's IP address this time. Minutes later, I got the first response to my change in relationship status: it was my sister back in Chandigarh.

What!!! Again? So who next?

Mom's asking if you got the new sim card?

I replied, *Hey, I'll call tonight. Once I am in my dorm, okay? Tell Mom I got the sim card. I still can't believe Mom, I mean, seriously she hid the sim in the chocolates she sent...woo...hooo:D and yeah, how's your groom hunting going along?*

Yes, you read it right. My Mom did send me a new sim card for my illegal cell phone. Cool, know? I know I am blessed.

The first page of our school diary categorically mentions that no electronics are allowed in dorms or on campus and these include iPods, PSPs, mobile phones...but then the last time I or perhaps most of my buddies followed the rules and regulations was probably in Class VI or VII, I think. You cannot survive with an official calling every weekend on only two prescribed numbers, can you?

The entire female population in my family is icy cool. Nidhi, my elder sister, is perhaps the only female around who has been strong enough to accept that her brother is a guy, a chauvinist, a hormone-driven pig. I love Nidhi. She is so beneficial after all—emotionally she guides, financially she supports and hormonally her friends contribute. Need I say more?

Nidhi always had an eye for my eye-popping acts. It was

she who caught me watching porn the first time in Class V; a lecture followed. Her sternness relaxed the next time she caught me sneaking into her room early morning when her friends had a sleepover. I was in Class VII then. Those long legs and short shorts—I won't forget you Ritika (her best friend). She was the first one to notice the nail-marks on my shoulder when I returned home last summer. 'Mosquitoes in hostel,' is what I told her. 'Female mosquitoes bite hard,' she had replied. I had guiltily laughed. I went clubbing with her during the last December holidays; it helps when you are with a twenty-four-year-old young lady.

And me, I am not that näive either—a six-foot frame supported by natural, silky black hair with a tinge of brown. I owe my sun-kissed complexion and athletic built to years of swimming and basketball. My underwater stroke (if there is any) is the best in a co-ed pool. The FCUK frames help in generating the intellectual boy persona. The bushy eyebrows perfectly compliment the thick sideburns. I shave often, my face I mean. It helps maintain the 'clean' boy image. Some people here think I am self-conceited and to them my only reply is, 'I respect you'.

𝔐

The stark reality still lay bare in front of me—I was single. Nidhi's comment had left me thinking. Who next?

3

He Still Lives and Lusts

It expands in extremes—fear and joy.
It burns with zeal—so strong and thick,
Water the plants, water the roads—just be quick.

'Boza, better be quick,' I said to myself as I sat waiting in the editorial room. 'Who could be next?' I wondered! Suddenly the expansion began (it was a situation of fear and joy, both).

I had to detoxify my body lest I wanted a burning pain. I had to let out the acid rain. I could now literally feel the fumes bubbling on the funnel tip. No more! I ran to the male laboratory, closing the door in haste.

'Fifth period over,' an almost supersonic voice boomed out on the speaker placed conveniently just above the lab door.

'They won't even let us pee in peace,' I heard a junior comment as he opened the door while I walked out in the same breath.

'We should write an article on how these speakers and the loud voice cause us stress, even if they work like neat alarm clocks,' I heard Chimmy's voice rise over the after-period babble in the corridor. Talk of irony!

'Turn it in this Saturday,' I said as I walked past her.

Surprisingly I didn't get any 'you womanizer' looks, nor did I have to answer any inquiry about the infamous evening between Rhea and me by the random classmates and teammates I hi-fived on the way. Even Rhea's best friend didn't eye me like a jailor ready to convict a rapist, as I had thought, when I saw her right outside the editorial room.

I was safe.

Ouch! Rhea was actually sweet.

But I am diabetic.

Chapter closed.

'I told you not to go, ass,' Boza boomed as soon as I entered the room.

'But p...'

She cut me, 'You know how the IT department randomly picks up abandoned laptops,' in a lecturing tone.

'I had to pee, okay,' I said.

'Again, please. Oh, you had to pee,' she brushed off the little embarrassment on her face. 'There is some important stuff in here,' she offered in explanation now.

'Yeah, your semi-naked pictures with the Tibetan Tarzan back home,' I announced.

'You dog,' she looked outraged.

'Oh and I had only randomly guessed,' I said with devious eyes.

She laughed, I laughed, problem solved.

'So how does it feel to be single?' she asked in a teasing voice, a few minutes later.

'My heart can survive the emotional trauma, but my hand! I don't know if it can bear the physical exhaustion after such a long time?' I replied in the same tone.

'Jerk,' she exclaimed.

'That's what I am talking about,' the jerk said, showing her the jerk(ing).

'Aaryan, just zip it up. Okay,' she said, asking me to literally shut up.

'It needs air….my mouth, yaar,' I winked at her. It was so easy talking crap with her.

'Fine, unzip and practise till you get perfect,' she said sarcastically and closed her laptop.

'Okay, cholly,' I said in a puppy-like voice. She smiled and opened her laptop again.

Thank God, my passport to bunk the next two periods wasn't taking off, the visa being the permission the editor enjoyed; official bunk, she called it.

'What took you so long anyway?' I questioned, starting a conversation I knew that wouldn't end even as the French and Psychology periods would.

'Nothing, just finalizing the country and all,' she replied. I gave a puzzled look, 'The country?'

'Oh, the Model United Nations. Hey,' she paused, 'why don't you come along?'

❦

Sixth Period
Editing nothing,
discussing everything.

Me to she. 'I feel like a motel—temporary glorification of act and action followed by excruciating solitude.'
She to me: 'God, Aaryan, you can only think of action, not attraction.'
Me to she: 'Newton said every action has an equal and opposite reaction.'

She to me: 'That wasn't even relevant. Come along for the MUN.'
Me to she: 'Now, is that relevant?'
She to me: 'It is actually.'
Me to she: 'Is it? Go on...'
She to me: 'Imagine you get to go three days out of school.'
Me to she: 'And nights?'
She to me: 'Shut up, you let it be.'

Seventh Period
In between, mastered randomness.

Me to she: 'I miss Rhea—I miss her hair, her eyes, her smile, her lips—juicy, smeared with peach lip gloss.'
She to me: 'Exactly, that's why I am saying, 'Come along'. There will be girls, girls from all around—north, south, east and west. You name it and they have it—the beauties, the high heels and the short skirts, the tight hair buns and the loosely buttoned formal shirts.'
Me to she: 'Don't mind, but you sound like the secretary of a Bangkok-based pimp.'
She to me: 'Just come along, man. I need you around when I am surrounded by hot guys.'
Me to she: 'Now we are talking. But I am sorry.'
She to me: 'Fine, get up and park your ass in class; no more helping you to bunk.'

Eighth Period
Helpless high tide,
forced to reside (in class).

She to me: 'Disappear. If the principal comes, I am not responsible.'

Me to she: 'Okay, my friend-turned-foe, I'll go.'

She to me: 'You can stay, perhaps for long.'

Me to she (salivating like a dog): 'How long?'

She to me: 'Till the competition; a month.'

Me to she: 'You know my soft point, my dear friend.'

She to me: 'First you sneer, now I am dear.'

Me to she: 'Booze, let loose.'

She to me: 'Great, it's you, Kabir, Shazia and me then.'

Me to she: 'But what do you want in return?'

She to me (shocked): 'Aaryan, that's the limit. How can you even talk like this?'

Me to she (embarrassed): 'I am sorry.'

She to me: 'Actually, I really like the new Ferrari cologne your sister sent you last week.'

Me to she: 'And my Mom thinks that you are a saint.'

She to me: 'I am saintly, mostly.'

Me to she: 'Yes, mostly.'

She to me: 'Perhaps you will be thanking me later; you never know when Cupid will strike.'

I smiled, she smiled, problem solved.

This was friendship in its most deadliest form, after all. 'Okay,' I said and got back to the most laborious activity—sleeping.

What I didn't know then was that a decision today was going to change my tomorrow.

For the night out, I won't be able to sleep.

Of girls from all directions, I would cross national boundaries. And Cupid would celebrate for I was going to lose my heart. Only to live in love.

4

He Lives and Likes

Model United Nations

She asked me to come closer.
She held me tightly with her hands and like a goddess, ordered
me to relax.
Next she moved her hands to engulf my neck.
I protested, but she undid the top button of my crisp new
formal shirt.

'This won't take much time if you cooperate,' she assured me
again.

I could feel her breath heavily on my face. Her breath
smelled of strawberry; her perfume was the subtle shade of
Indian spice. Ahhh...the silky touch of the soft material and
her hands!

She worked upon me with great precision, mastering every
move with acute detailing.

Now her hand slid down to my stomach. She adjusted the
string according to the need. I had started to feel the heat. She
gave the final touch by adjusting my belt in accordance with
her earlier move.

'Perfect length,' she exclaimed.

'Yes, to a great extent,' I replied, wiping off the beads of sweat.

And before I knew, Boza, my best friend, had tied my tie for me.

'I will suffocate to death; it is boiling in here,' my voice rose with the temperature. The small audience of Boza, Kabir, and Shazia just threw looks at me, instead of the anticipated shillings and coins.

7.30 a.m.: The merciless sun shining with all its might.

Batra's borrowed Blackberry suit just fit. The school's Honda CRV nowhere in sight. Our supposed teacher in-charge still calling it a night. This definitely wasn't the ideal beginning to the day.

'Kabir dude, how do you manage this formal futility? This tie is so tied up,' I asked the MUN veteran.

He briefly smiled, a no-nonsense senior, I analysed.

'How do I look?' Boza asked, as she saw me checking out Shazia, our junior, the next minute.

'Are you officially asking me to check you out?' I joked, trying to hide my arrest.

Boza had told me over breakfast that her day had begun at 5 a.m. with a hot-water bubble bath, followed by the application of a face pack she had smuggled through the salon-cum-parlour on the campus. Now, as I was officially asked to judge her efforts, I couldn't help but just stare at the transformed delicate beauty to 'delegate' beauty.

With a just-above-the-knee-length black skirt, a formal pink shirt unbuttoned by the count of two from the top and one from the bottom, a zero power frame and high stilettos, a tight bun complimenting her sharp nose and inherent chinky eyes coupled with a slender body frame—I gave her high marks. Something else was rising high too, down under.

The next second, two sexually distinct voices could be heard—the loud masculine horn of the CRV and the heavenly (I mean heavily) accented, 'I'm sorry, I am late,' feminine shout from Chloe, our French teacher who was to accompany us as the teacher in-charge, for the next three days.

I quickly checked myself in my illegal Nokia E-71's double camera—the silky hair, straightened today with Boza's hair-straightening rod, fell on my FCUK frames, the light pink shirt, the neck-kissing tie—the modern debater looked thus achieved.

Kabir was checking out his appearance too. Chloe had this effect on every carbon-based life on the campus, the envy of the X-gene pool; the salivation in admiration from the Y-gene one.

To begin with, she was all of twenty-three. She treated us like young adults and never minded being addressed by her first name. She was a goddess, for her name was religiously taken in the boys' bathroom every morning and late at night; they hand-worshipped her. Her famous seven piercing(s) were like the seven mystical wonders for a typical B.N. World School's student; five wonders were visible to all, only a few claimed to have known about the two hidden (un)obvious holes.

Today she had worn a low-back cut peach suit, proudly flaunting off her butterfly tattoo.

'You look great, ma'am,' I heard Kabir say as we all sat in the car.

'Thank you,' she smiled back.

'Bhaiya, India Habitat Centre, Lodhi Road,' I informed the driver who was busy checking out our teacher in the rear-view mirror. Sitting parallel to him, I could see the reluctance in his eyes which now had no choice, but to see everywhere but in her direction for the next one hour.

The journey to IHC passed as uneventfully as the last month had, with no incident which could entertain, and with no girl to entertain, it moved at its leisured will, sailing through the occasional high currents. Rhea was history now; so was the preparation to plan dates in and out of hostel or to play basketball.

'Finally,' Boza announced, as our car stopped in front of the main complex. We all got down.

'This is big stuff,' Shazia, the shy junior, commented eyeing the grand, aristocratic building.

'Wait till you get inside,' said Kabir, as he signalled to me to help with the massive model.

The model in question was a voluptuous, young, glowing, glittered body. It was to be presented in the gallery as part of the MUN. It (not she) is formally called a country profile, which is an artistic representation about your country's social, political and cultural background.

One look at the model and we knew our labour and pain had delivered a healthy, oversized baby. The art department along with the help of the students back at the school had been bribed with the prospect of bunking classes to successfully convert our visually-depressing vision into a practical reality.

'Easy; slowly boys,' Chloe huffed and puffed as she bent down with us to place the model on the ground. Her *dupatta* fell in the action. In the process that followed I touched her hand twice, elbowed once into one of the round, firm, beautiful ball and unwillingly got a peek-a-boo inside at what was trapped and aching to be unstrapped.

'Phew, this was hard,' she said, getting up as the curtain (*dupatta*) fell on the free show.

That was hard and so was something down there. I

adjusted my boxer on the pretext of brushing off the glitter on my just-fit pants.

'Smile,' said Boza, clicking away to glory for her first Facebook album of the day—Oops, caught red-handed, I inferred from the disgusted look on her face a second later. Damn the digital clarity for displaying my expressions.

'I'll go for registration with Shazia,' Chloe said.

'I'll come along,' Kabir quickly added and asked me and Boza to keep the country profile in the gallery.

'I hope you know where it is?' he asked with a fake politeness.

'It should be, I think, inside the complex,' he glared at me and left after the two.

'What?' I asked Boza as we bent down to pick up the model.

'You are imbalanced,' she replied.

'Yes, hormonally there is an overdose,' my joke was based on the past experience and the show Boza's unbuttoned-by-the-two shirt provided, when bending.

Hard work pays, I learned practically and visually.

'Stop staring at my bust, you opportunist.' Three years with me were enough for her to recognize the reason behind my after-every-twenty-minute expression.

'Sorry, bust, I mean best friend,' I replied innocently.
She laughed, I laughed, problem solved.

❧

'We have some serious booty business here,' I whistled, looking at the fifty-odd pairs of covered-only-by-necessity, shining, female legs. Was this a dream? No, it wasn't, for I don't generally dream about some seventy-odd pairs of thankfully covered male legs alongside. Still Boza had been true to her word. There were many pulsating opportunities around.

'Not now,' Boza popped the testosterone bubble, as if reading my mind. We placed the profile on the nearest empty table. She bent sideways this time, intentionally I think.

'Aaryan, look for our school name,' she paused, 'only for our school name.' Her low thoughts about me were the high point of the bond we shared.

So sick,
still we clicked.

I started to scan the linearly put tables catering to a variety of models in all shapes and sizes being presented by probable models in the same shape and sizes.

'Over here,' I heard Boza shoot from the south end. I went back to where our model was kept.

Boza seemed to have no intention of coming and helping me, lest her formal attire faced an early retirement. With all the force I could muster, I picked up the model single-handedly. The just-fit suit and the heavy model were making it all the more difficult to walk without brushing or hitting someone, or to be more ruthlessly honest, pushing people as I managed a few drunkard steps. The liberal verbose of 'Sorry, excuse me; watch out; my fault,' drained me of all courtesy midway through the obstacle path. Ignorance is bliss! Thus reaffirmed, I now moved recklessly, turning deaf to the slurs being hurled at me, partially blind I already was, with the model covering my face, allowing me only minor peripheral vision.

'Here, let me help you,' an accented yet homely, pristine yet uplifting voice vibrated in my eardrums. A second and my heart skipped a beat. I felt uplifted many times together. An extremely fair hand, dipped in the colour of love, firmly held the model from the other side.

A major part of her face remained hidden mysteriously by the heavy ball and with every step we took, my desire to become Sherlock Holmes increased. I inhaled deeply, trying to take in the fragrance of the helpful soul. Her scent was unfamiliar yet it invoked warm emotions.

Either it was the high heels, or she was naturally tall, I could not tell. Wearing a red half-sleeved shirt and a dark coloured skirt, she moved along with an inborn grace. The extremely fair arm seemed to dazzle my bespectacled eye, while the dolphin-hanging gold bracelet shimmered less in comparison to the aura she generated around her to engulf me. The side view which had revealed all this so far now posited Boza in its periphery. We had reached, almost...

I cleared my throat to say, 'Just here,' my voice in comparison to hers was not even worth an audible mention.

'Alright,' she replied. We started to keep the model in the designated area. I had to sit on my hind in the Indian-seat style to place the model on the low table.

'Thanks a ton,' Boza said, not giving me time to even get up and do the needful, after she had helped ME.

'No problem,' I heard melody at its musical best again.

'Aaryan,' I heard Boza call for me. I was still in the uncomfortable position of standing half bent, sitting half standing. Somehow I just couldn't see her face. I wanted to, but I felt as if I was stuck in this position by super-glue. My pretending to fix some unbreakable part, which apparently must have broken, rescued me from the obvious awkwardness of not facing or thanking her first.

'I'll see you around,' the guitar struck on a lighter note and I saw her lower body turn; obviously her upper body would accompany her. Any second and she would go away from me as abruptly as she had come. As she took the first step forward, my heart sank downward (remember the position) and then she stopped. Something metallic, small, golden and shining had fallen near my foot. It was the small dolphin from her bracelet. There was no escape now; she bent down to pick it.

In the same action, I straightened my back and got up. Phew. Minor escape...but was it one? She suddenly got up and bang, she stood in front of me!

❦

We were walking towards the auditorium; the inaugural ceremony was to start soon.

'Kabir messaged; they all are already there,' Boza's vocals beeped, after her illegal cell phone had. My ears heard her though my eyes still scanned the surroundings for the helpful girl who was turning me helpless with every passing moment.

'There aren't any cute asses here; anyway leave that. Who was that girl?' Boza suddenly turned the spotlight on me.

'Yes, we will meet Kabir and Shazia there,' I answered, remembering the last words I had paid heed to.

'Huh?' she was obviously startled.

'Boza, who was that girl?' I asked softly, repeating the question she had asked me a minute ago.

'Aaryan, are you alright? That's just what I had asked'

'What?' now I was startled.

'Who was that girl?' she asked again.

'Yes, that's what I said. I mean asked; I mean who was that girl?'

'Aaryan, stop,' she said hotly and followed it with a physical blow. She held me from my waist and turned me around. Boza was silently studying my face.

'What?' I asked uncomfortably.

'Nothing, I thought I saw a wish, but it's not there,' she

said, ruffling my hair playfully to indicate she knew what I knew.

'There's nothing...not till now,' I cleverly covered up, pausing in between to help her understand that I also knew what she knew about me.

Through the corner of my eye, *I saw her grin in sympathy. Through the corner of her eye, she saw me smile in helplessness: we had a problem at hand.*

🐾

'Quick, grab a seat wherever you can,' Kabir barked on the phone. Yes, ninety-nine per cent of us do believe in hidden cellular operations.

'Whoosh him,' I whispered in Boza's free ear as I scanned for empty seats in the dimly lit, overcrowded two-storeyed auditorium.

'You are late,' he shouted loudly, taking advantage of the hoots that had engulfed the auditorium which worked better than the surround sound.

'Thanks, man. Only you are destined to see,' I spoke loudly so that he could hear, while poor Boza digested the verbal food for thought. Suddenly the dim lights turned a two shade dimmer; I could hardly see Boza now.

'We are in the balcony. Give our id cards later,' Boza's shout made me identify her position.

'Fine,' she cut her phone in one swift action; the next being holding my hand and walking towards the crowded aisle. 'Just,' her voice drained from the applause that came out of nowhere. She pulled me down and I collided with a body, which was already seated in the centre aisle.

'Sorry,' I aimlessly shouted to the faintly visible outline which had inched away from me. 'Must be a girl,' I whispered to Boza, whose hand I was still holding.

'You player, you are talking about a girl while you are holding another's hand,' she accused jokingly and before I could reply, the spotlight fell on the stage and the compère began.

Two minutes into the speech and I found my thoughts drifting back to the enchanting encounter.

Sniff? 'I can smell her,' I whispered right into Boza's right ear, as she sat, intently listening or rather checking out the hunky compere.

'You can smell her?' she asked, without looking at me. So she was checking him out.

'Yes,' I replied again.

'God, you really are a dog,' she said.

Perhaps I was dreaming too intently. Tired of guessing, I decided to pay attention to the proceedings. The next round of applause announced the arrival of the chief guest on stage, to recite or rather read out a speech.

'Welcome future leaders,' he began. 'As you all know, MUN or Model United Nations is an academic simulation of how the United Nations works. You, the delegates of 130 countries, students of more than eighty schools in India and ten schools abroad, will propose, oppose and form alliances.' '*Over coffee,*' somebody sitting on the seats in the vicinity spoke loudly and we all burst out laughing.

When the auditorium is dark,
the audience will bark.

The chief guest ignored the sudden commotion, 'You are the future of the country; you, acting as delegates, will debate.' '*Or date,*' I heard somebody shout from behind and the same cycle of laughter followed. 'You will be sensitized about the issues that burn the world today. You will need to gang up for action.'

'*Gang-bang,*' I shouted suddenly, pedalling the ongoing cycle. Boza poked me her elbow. The chief guest paused briefly, unable to find the epicentre of the ongoing tremor in the dark atmosphere. He resumed again, 'You will deliberate over policies, analyze and scrutinize, but be prepared for some of you might get framed in visually and physically heated conflicts.'

'Oh my God, another MMS scandal,' I kept this chuckling thought to myself.

'...Some may benefit from strengthened bonds.'

'*Over Facebook*,' Boza whispered in my ear.

'Lastly, I suggest, request and warn you to prevent and use protection against political favours.'

'*In all flavours,*' a guy, sitting right behind me spoke in an audible volume for the whole balcony to hear, the laughter that followed filled the whole auditorium.

'Thank you,' the chief guest ended his speech before time. Mission accomplished—'united' team.

'The next half hour passed mocking and at times marvelling at the beautiful acts put up by the host school. Finally it was time for action. The gloom returned to glory. Sniff! Before I could adjust my eyes to the brightness again, my nose was alerted by a recently inhaled fragrance. I was about to mention the same to Boza, but she seemed to know it already. Her nudge in my stomach was testimony of it.

'What?' I exclaimed, following her gaze. So I actually am a dog—a real good sniffer dog. The helpful girl was actually around but what left me verbally and physically paralysed was the fact that she had been the female who had collided and inched away from me. During the entire inaugural ceremony, she had sat right next to me and I didn't know. My eyes couldn't eye, my heart couldn't feel. Damn it!

'Hi again,' she smiled to me.

'Thank You. Oh sorry, I mean 'hi' and sorry again for the 'thank you'. Oh, I mean thanks and hey,' I stuttered and stammered, still glued to my seat. She, Boza and almost the rest of the audience had got up.

'Okay,' she said and smiled, visibly embarrassed.

'He is just a bit nervous actually,' Boza said in my defence as she kicked me like someone would kick a dog, asking it to get up and move. I got the signal; I am a good sniffer, a trained dog after all.

'By the way, I am Boza,' she extended her hand.

'Ishita, delegate of France,' she said, extending her hand. 'And you?' she asked me, after she had shook hands with her.

I couldn't decide what was redder—her nail-paint or my face. 'Aaryan,' I said, extending my hand without even thinking about the sudden sweat on my palm in the air-conditioned auditorium.

'So, which country are you representing?' she enquired, breaking our first physical embrace.

'Gabon,' I replied, managing to net her words which fluttered like butterflies.

'Oh, where is it?' she asked us collectively.

'Right next to you; oh, you mean the location? It is in Africa,' I found myself blurting.

She sensed my nervousness, 'So, is this your first time?'

'Yes,' Boza replied for me again.

'Which committee are you on?' she now directed all her questions at her; obviously a tongue-tied guy wouldn't make the best conversation.

'I am in ECOSOC, Aaryan is in General Assembly,' Boza informed her.

I said a quick silent prayer. 'What about you?' I asked her.

'Me?' she was evidently surprised at the mute movie turning into a musical. 'I am in General Assembly too,' she smiled briefly. I smiled back, thinking on how quickly prayers are answered.

'Great, I'll see you guys around then,' she said and left.

'So, Aaryan this definitely seems to be your first time,' Boza said teasingly, with an underlying hint of reality. This was my first time—the first time Aaryan the player had been hit and hit bad.

'Yes, Boza,' I side-hugged her in realization.

I laughed, she laughed, problem solved.

5

He Lives, Likes and Likes Some More

Eyes are meant to see, not hypnotize. Lips are used to let out what you feel, not seal one's monosyllabic ambitions. Cheeks and skin are meant to give shape and texture, not become the reason to drool. Expressions are meant to signify, not turn into a portal of purity and dignity. Plastic vanity can brighten many an ordinary face; only a few rely on serenity and simplicity that strike the human eye, leaving one dumbstruck on how God creates, nurtures and protects us to symbolize and marvel. As I sat in the committee room at a sizeable distance from her, realization began to set in.

She was the Chosen One.

'Delegate of Finland, delegate of France.'

'Present and voting,' she spoke, raising the placard bearing her country's name as the attendance was being taken.

'Delegate of Gabon?'

Silence!

'Delegate of Gabon?'

'Present and voting,' I quickly responded as the speakers blasted the name of the country I had worked upon for the whole of last month.

'Please be attentive,' he warned.

'But the delegate is in shock at the prevailing agenda that rules our discussion,' I stood up and spoke, hoping she would hear. She obviously had, for I was the only fool to stand up and turn the tables against the esteemed judging panel, popularly known as the 'Chair', even before the verbal battle had begun.

'Curiously concerned,' the Director, another member of the judging panel commented as if blowing the war trumpets. I pulled back my chair to sit again.

To reveal a little secret, I myself wasn't sure of the agenda the General Assembly was going to discuss. For all I care, was that...

She glanced at me briefly
I looked at her longingly,
so she believed.
Finally relieved.

❧

'The next meeting shall begin after twenty minutes.'

'Finally,' I murmured and got up to move.

'Delegate of Gabon, if you could please honour your seat with the grace of your physical being,' said the Director, successfully turning some fifty-odd heads towards me.

I wasn't embarrassed and I would have thought of revenge, had her head not been in the fifty heads that turned to me.

She briefly stared, yes, again.

'We adjourn,' the Director said.

Suddenly commotion engulfed the room. Everyone got up and almost brisk walked towards the door. Two hours of constant scrutiny, debate and a highly formal atmosphere, where even farting required permission, had drained all the Delegates.

I caught up with Ishita at the door. This was my chance—the

ideal time for the third impression. 'Ishita *Je T'aime*,' I whispered into her ear from behind. She turned around, surprised! One look into her eyes, to be more specific, one look at my reflection in her eyes and I realized why every love ballad in Bollywood had eyes as its heart. Had she stood there for another minute, my grin would have transformed into the curvature of a semicircle.

'Excuse moi,' she replied in her country's language.

'*Bonjour*,' I said.

'What?' she said, returning to the familiar language.

'I am sorry but my French exhausts here,' I grinned apologetically. It was a lie which would remain as one; it was all part of the plan.

'So, do you know the meaning of what you whispered in my ear in the first place?' Her tone had a very subtle shade of surprise.

'Actually,' I paused throwing in the trump card, 'my friend told me...that's how you greet young, intelligent, smart, fair, tall, elegant, naturally beautiful girls in France and you are representing that country. So I thought...' I replied with all the forced innocence.

'Well, if you think I'll buy that, then you are mistaken,' she stated in a matter-of-fact tone.

'Nobody is asking you to buy anything; just accept it,' I said softly.

I saw her lower her eyes. Was it an illusion or her extremely fair cheeks had just developed a tinge of the colour of love? Without saying anything, she started to move.

I fell into step, just by her side. The other delegates were walking by, in front, behind, everywhere around us. We reached the end of the corridor and climbed down the stairs, leading to the reception area, in silence.

'Accept what?' she suddenly asked, on the last step.

'My greetings,' I said in response to my first salutation to her.

'You know what it means, right?' she asked seriously.

'I told you what my friend told me,' I replied, faking a genuine frame. My cell phone suddenly vibrated violently and I jumped, 'Excuse me,' I said, turning around and hissing into the phone. 'Kabir I am busy. No, okay. Bye.'

Damn Kabir, damn Boza, damn Shazia—they all could wait. I had just offered her the bait.

'Yes, so what was I saying?' I asked her, after turning around.

'Well, for starters, you need to brush up your acting skills,' she said after scrutinizing my expressions for a few moments.

'Fine...guilty as charged,' I surrendered to the clever, helpful, beautiful and sweet—her description could go on and on and on.

'*Je T'aime* is 'I love you' in French,' I said slowly, emphasizing on each word.

'Your trick was old,' she merrily announced.

'You seem to be in situations like this often,' I said, clearly flirting with her.

'You should thank your stars,' she said, smiling.

'Because I met you?' I replied, piling on the flirts.

'No, because I endorse Gandhi,' she said, crackling her knuckles and folding them into a sweet namaste.

'You know I have a real good dialogue here,' I said, trying to reciprocate.

'If I guess this right, you support my resolution,' she spelled out the deal.

A resolution was the end process of any Model United Nations meeting. The delegate who drafted it was definitely considered to be tactful, diplomatic and charming. It was no surprise that most of the times, girls drafted the resolutions—a first-hand experience on how they lobby.

'Done! Guess the line,' I said.

'You were about to say that it's okay, if you would have slapped me, at least you would have got to touch me this way,' she smiled after a mild dramatization of a B-grade Bollywood movie.

'To Bollywood,' I said, raising my id card in a toast.

'To Bollywood,' she repeated and smiled.

'So where are you from?' I asked her the first important question.

National calls through cell phones are subsidized anyway and then Skype is always there, so I wouldn't have minded a Nagaland or Kankyakumari, though her accent indicated towards a Metro largely, maybe Mumbai.

'Isn't the accent a give away?' she asked. It was her turn to play.

'If I win this guess, you have coffee with me at the American Diner outside,' I announced the deal now.

'You know, I still can't believe you are the same guy who looked like he would shit in his pants any second, back there in the auditorium,' she smiled diabolically.

The words stung. 'Well, if I say it was you who made me nervous, you would think I am flirting,' I said, digesting or gulping down the last few emotions.

'Isn't that what you have been doing since...' she checked her watch, '...the past ten minutes.'

'Oh, c'mon,' I raised my hands in mock protest. 'Actually this was just a warm-up.'

She smiled. 'So I don't make you nervous now?' she asked a tricky question.

'You are from Mumbai?' I asked, dodging her question.

'Mumbai. There goes your coffee,' she said, making a sad face.

'Huh? Not Mumbai, then where? Delhi?' I asked frantically

as my deal had fallen out. Coffee would need a new way.

'I am from Singapore,' she said.

'Singapore!' I exclaimed loudly, as if it was an omen.

'Yeah. Why?' She sensed the surprise in my voice.

'No, I mean, I thought, you were a local.' The shattered dreams were scattered and every passing second they seemed to bruise me.

'No, I am not local; I am, umm...international,' she said and laughed, while I forced a smile.

'So, why don't I make you nervous now?' she asked me again.

You just make me helpless, sad, dejected, rejected and all the synonyms of 'lonely' now. Still I couldn't give up. One glance at her face recharged me emotionally and mentally.

Physically the hormonal rise,
never let the need arise.

'Well, you have been around for the past two hours and...' checking my Tissot, especially jerking my hand so that she could take notice of what I pretended to not flaunt, 'fourteen minutes to be precise and sometimes, they say, all it takes is a moment to connect,' I said, adding a layer on the already layered flirt-cake.

'But what if all the routes of connection are jammed?'

Did she not have an affinity toward cakes? I could bake a pie too.

'Well, there always is the DTH service,' I said, digging deeper into the wit-resource in me.

'DTH, as in direct to home?' she asked the question I had prepared my answer for.

'No, DTH here is direct to heart,' I said, hoping she would laugh this time.

She just smiled again.

Why was I continuing to flirt with her even though her last signal talked about jammed connections? Perhaps because of the spirit of the B.N. World School, the heart transcends all geographical boundaries as we had always been taught; it was time now to practise.

'Okay, bye!' she said abruptly and started to move with the same level of abruptness.

'Hey, wait,' I called out to her.

She turned to say, 'I have to meet friends,' and turned away again.

'Didn't you just make one?' I raised my volume, at which a few people turned their heads.

She kept on walking and with each step, the mounting of the feeling of dejection followed the rejection. As she reached for the door leading to the grounds outside, she turned and literally shouted, 'That's the cheesiest line I have ever heard.'

I quickly jogged up to her. 'It,' I huffed, 'may be the cheesiest, but it was the easiest,' said I, giving the puppy-eyed look—a look generally reserved for distant and extreme situations. Damn, she lived far away anyway!

'Aaryan, the only problem is...' she said, before looking at her watch quickly. The twenty-minute break was nearing its end; the reception area was getting crowded with every passing second.

'The only problem is,' she repeated, 'I hate people who flirt because love itself seems so lame, I don't believe in relationships and yeah, I am sort of totally allergic to your type of cheese.' Saying so, she quickly walked out to find her teammates, leaving me shocked.

Some time later...

'Where were you in the first break?' Boza interrogated me.

'Just hanging around,' I lied with confidence. Years of bunking religiously in school had turned me into a priest of fibs for such situations.

We were moving along in the lunch line. The twenty-one-dish buffet attractively spread in the sprawling lawns had been successful enough in stopping me from following Ishita and getting cheesed away yet again.

The second meeting had been pretty dull with only a sprinkle of entertainment in the form of the delegate of India, who was caught sleeping and another delegate, who burped on the mike, forgetting that courtesy as a word was coined for some reason. I myself was busy playing hide-and-seek—my eyes were busy seeking the face she was trying to hide. I spied her four times but she cheated and never reciprocated.

Towards the end of the meeting, my new-found comrade and adjacent partner, the delegate of Hungary, a decent guy from Chennai, helped me not to look at my watch tick slowly by some serious game of tic-tac-toe. The only time I paid attention was when any country starting with the letters F and G were called out to the podium.

'I can't believe you are taking all this so seriously. I thought you would be bunking here too or worse, you must be following the France girl,' Boza said, surprised at my sincerity.

'Ishita. She is Ishita,' I cut in. Nobody, not even my best friend, had the right to call her 'the France girl'. Fine, I was just getting hyper but she gave me the high.

'Okay, chill,' she said.

'Yeah,' I said, adjusting my tie and trying to camouflage my emotional discomfort coupled with the physical discomfort.

'Uncomfortable with the tie?' she asked.

'You bet,' I replied.

'Here, let me help you,' she offered, keeping her plate on a nearby empty table.

I had no choice but to agree. 'Go slow okay? I like it long,' I said mischievously.

'Sure thing,' she said and pulled the tie string in a really swift move. I was left gasping... No that was too decent for the situation. In all honesty, I was choking!

'Booze,' I said, coughing and juggling with the plate in the other hand.

A few heads turned towards us and contrary to expectations, ignored the ongoing drama for reasons best known to them. I still think it was the extra food to be finished in the less time available.

I choked in disappointment. She finally let me loose.

'I saw you standing in the reception area with Ishita. The name is Ishita (she imitated me) and don't abandon me during break ever again, even if the girl in question is taller, sexier and super hot,' she thundered.

She smiled, I smiled, problem solved.

'The cottage cheese (*paneer*) here is no good,' Boza said ten minutes later as we sat enjoying our lunch. Ishita wasn't around, not in my view at least. But what about her intention and attention?

'Ishita's last reply to me was, "I am allergic to cheese",' I mocked in reply.

'So she can't stay away from the conversation even for ten minutes now,' she faked anger and laughed.

'She can stay away from the mind, but what about the heart?' I replied back, laughing.

'Aaryan, c'mon,' she pressed, getting serious all of a sudden.

'What?' I protested.

'I want to know what all happened in the last meeting,' she urged.

'Fine, we started with the role call, before we were asked to select the agenda,' I started.

'No, not the committee meeting, I mean, your meeting—Ishita and you,' she said.

'Oh that? That is a long, l...o...n...g story,' I said, prolonging the 'long'.

'We still have time,' she said, looking at her watch.

'But, what about the ice cream?' I asked playfully. It was fun to see the curiosity level in Boza's actions and words rise.

'Fine, we will take some ice cream quickly and sit on the stairs near the door to the reception area,' she said and got up.

'Let me eat at least,' I said, playing with the international *khichdi* on my plate.

'Aaryan, don't even think of having the sausage. It has noodles all around, and eek, some white thing on its one end,' she said, wrinkling her nose, after commenting on my plate's inhabitants.

'Oh that is dip, not di...'

'Shut up,' she said and snatched away the spoon from my hand. 'Move,' she ordered.

'But my back doesn't ache,' I said lamely. I simply didn't want to go through the ordeal of telling a story which began with 'I love you' and sweet nothings and ended on allergies and cheese.

'That wasn't funny,' she said, giving me the Aaryan-I-will-kill-you-next look.

'Okay,' I said, getting up and trying to ease her temperature with ice cream.

There were so many flavours to savour. I finally zeroed on choco-chip while Boza scooped a white, thick, almost-watery mass (melted vanilla).

'Let's sit,' I said, after we managed to fill our plates with the ice cream that would last the sweet encounter which was waiting to be told.

Ten minutes later, we were sitting on the stairs. Another five minutes later, I was midway through the narrative and the five minutes thereafter marked the end.

'Oh my God,' Boza paused after every word, giving a three-word response to the odd 3000-word story.

'What?' I wanted her to clarify her apprehensive or appreciative stand.

'You actually used you-just-made-a-friend line again?' she said in a disappointed tone.

'With her, it's different,' I reasoned.

'Rhea was unique; she is different,' Boza commented.

'Yaar...she is sitting in the first row and I am way behind. We hardly can see each other, leave aside talking,' I said, spelling out the physical problem (I mean distance).

'Oh *yeh dooriyan*,' Boza dramatized, flaunting her Indian knowledge (which was limited to Bollywood).

'Yes, *yeh dooriyan*. Where are the others?' I asked, trying to change the topic.

'Why don't you chit-pass with her?' Boza suggested, not letting me change it.

'What is that?' I weakly asked.

'Aaryan, you can pass chits to fellow delegates through the messengers, I mean the people who are standing on the side aisles; passing little chits and messages.'

I gave her a confused look.

'Were you seriously in there for the last meeting or not?' she asked me now, concerned.

'Bunking is a habit, not a necessity,' I retorted back.

'Well I did see the...as you say, messengers walk down the aisles,' I said, realizing how foolish I was to think that little pieces of paper feverishly being passed contained politically personal suggestions and proposals.

'I henceforth proclaim you the king of Dumdum land,' she joked, fishing out something from her pocket. 'Check this out,' she said in MTV-ish style.

I took the chit from her. It read:

Dear delegate of Gabon,

My heartiest greetings! Delegate, I feel a cup of coffee in my country's diner outside, during the next break, will help us decide the future of our alliance with respect to the problem at hand.

The delegate is available after the official hours through correspondence on the internet or on Facebook

—Rishabh Singh, Mumbai

Yours (if you want),
Delegate from United States of America

'Are you serious about this?' I couldn't believe what I had just read.

'*Ahan...*,' she beamed.

'Did you go? Don't the messengers read your chits...Who paid for the coffee and yeah, don't tell me you are ditching the Tarzan now?' I started the rapid-fire round.

'Easy man. No, I didn't go. He did not have a cute ass. Not my type and taste; not that I would have tasted it,' she quickly added on seeing my alarmed look working as the alarm. I gave her a sick look.

'And the messengers?' I inquired next.

'The messengers do read your chits, but most of them just

giggle and pass them on.'

'And the rest?'

'Give it to the international press here, for the newspaper that is printed daily.'

'Hmmm and where does this newspaper go?'

'To the delegates and teachers, even to schools sometimes,' she replied.

'Hmm...now that can be risky,' I observed.

'Risk is rewarding,' Boza said in between licks.

'Boza, stop licking the spoon; you look horny,' I said plainly. She apologetically grinned.

'So where is she from?' she asked.

'Who? Ishita?' I asked.

'Duh..,' she groaned.

'Oh, that is another problem. She is from Singapore,' I grimaced.

'*Yeh dooriyan*,' she dramatized again.

'I know, *yeh dooriyan*; it's just not possible. She stays so far.'

'She is near,' Boza's whisper cut me short.

'Singapore is near, very near,' I said sarcastically.

'But she is near; just turn around, idiot,' she hissed, doing the honour of turning me herself.

Ishita was walking towards us with a group of my committee people. She had a ton of files containing, I suspect, information on other countries and the ongoing topic, in her hand.

'Boy, she is taking this conference seriously,' I heard Boza remark.

In the usual habit of all boys, I adjusted my coat and ran my hand through my hair quickly, hoping or rather knowing she would notice; she just had to notice.

But she passed us without even throwing a look at me. I wouldn't have minded a stare, a glare, anything, just to show that I existed and she cared.

'Did she just not notice or deliberately decided not to notice?' Boza asked me, breaking the stabbing silence.

'Uh...I don't know but I want to know. Let's move,' I replied, trying to lick my wound.

We got up. Before I could tell Boza about the ointment that could treat my hurt, she found a new prescription altogether.

'Look, someone dropped this,' Boza said, bending down to pick up a book.

'Whatever,' I replied nonchalantly as I really didn't care. I was feeling as neglected as the poor, lonely abandoned book.

'Aaryan, I think you will need this,' Boza said with a new enthusiasm in her voice.

'What?' I questioned, confused.

She opened the book to its first page, pointing towards a very artistic handwriting. It read: *This book is gifted to Ishita Palithingal by Ramona Kaur.*

Was God playing games with me? Was this how it was supposed to be?

'She must have dropped this accidentally or perhaps...' Boza left her sentence open to interpretation.

'Booze, what book is it?' I asked as a rejuvenating pulse ran through my body.

'It's *A Walk to Remember*, by Nicholas Sparks,' she informed.

'Haven't heard of the book or the writer,' I told her honestly.

'You haven't?' she seemed shocked.

'Yeah, I haven't,' I told her.

'Aaryan, every girl reads Nicholas Sparks once she hits puberty. He is like Eric Segal's successor...there is a movie too based on this book,' she said, as if she was the spokesperson for the writer.

'So it means, Ishita likes romance—a girl, who thinks that flirting is lame, likes romantic novels. Hmmm...!'

'Yeah seemingly, otherwise why would she carry it with her, over here, of all the places?'

'So I'll return the book to her personally,' I said, feeling somewhat rejuvenated.

6

He Lives, Likes, Loves

'This has to be my walk for her to remember,' I muttered to myself as I walked back into the committee room to where she sat.

'Hey, Ishita,' I said confidently.

'Oh, hi!' she said, looking up.

'Delegates please be seated.' The rapporteur's voice blared through the speakers, blasting my chance again.

G…r…e…a…t! They want to resume talk just when I was about to begin mine. With a final grinding of the teeth (I hope it looked like a grimace at least), I headed towards my seat.

The final meeting for the day began.

After thirty minutes of constant staring and simultaneous debating (on how I should tell her that while she held captive my attention and my heart, in comparison I just had her small, little novel), I sat looking confused.

'Chit-pass Aaryan,' I suddenly remembered Boza's suggestion.

'But what if I got caught?'

'Risk is rewarding,' Boza's words hallucinated my memories again.

'You want to chit pass, don't you?' suddenly spoke the tic-tac-toe buddy (my adjacent partner), reading my mind.

'Me? No, not really. Maybe,' I said sheepishly. 'But dude, how did you guess?' I queried.

'You have been playing with your notepad for so long,' he pointed out.

'Oops! Well, yeah!' I grinned.

'As I far as I gauge these chits could not be related to the ongoing agenda of discussion here,' he went on.

'You seem to know everything,' I replied. Man, this person was seriously psyched.

'Well, not really, but I know this messenger here. I befriended her over lunch, you know. We still have two days to go and a lot of chits to pass,' he grinned proudly.

'Neat man,' I admitted.

'So, write freely. The girl on the left corner—signal to her once you're done writing,' he instructed me.

'Okay,' I said, looking around for his friend and my saviour—the double adjective conferred here happened to be a girl, who could be no more than fourteen, but dressed up to look sixteen.

'Perfect catch,' I whispered to the guy (I hadn't asked his name till now).

We both laughed a chauvinistic laugh and then I began to write.

Chit No. 1
From Me to She

Oh, delegate of France,
call it luck or chance or my vigilant stance.
Even though you are blissfully unaware,
about your belongings more than your looks.

'A Walk to Remember', I found a book.

—*Aaryan, delegate of Gabon*

Call it luck by chance, the messenger just happened to walk by as I finished folding the written chit. I signalled to her.

'Delegate of France, first row,' I whispered to my partner in crime and otherwise. I winked at her! She probably understood, for she merely smiled after going through the chit.

I smiled back in gratitude, adding a dose of flirt. She seemed to like the action as her next reaction was to walk up straight to Ishita, ignoring all the other chits she had in her hand.

I saw Ishita take the chit. She opened it next. She began reading it. Silently she scanned and searched around for her novel. Then she turned around to get a view of the whole room. Her eyes halted at me—time stood still for me and then she abruptly turned away.

She read the chit again, turned around again and her eyes stopped at me again, possibly seeing a different me—one who carelessly for the world, but carefully for her world, held his right ear to signify an apology. To others what might have been an attempt at digging the ear, for her it was a gesture which would pave and cement the relation that was to follow.

Love has its own sets of challenges and pains. Pain pays, for I saw her tear a chit and write something for somebody—guess what? That somebody was me.

Chit No. 2
She to Me

My poetry may not be so strong,
My first notion about your cheesy methods might have been
wrong.

What you have is not just a book;
It is a precious gift, which in ignorance I must have dropped,
and you like a God-sent angel on the scene popped.
Do enlighten me on where it lay,
I feel today is a very lucky day.
I ask you to forgive and forget.
Mom never let me keep a pet (sorry, but I wanted to rhyme
it so desperately).

> —*From the delegate who forgives*

I began to frantically write my reply again.

Chit No. 3
Me to She

Oh delegate of France, your poetic reply made me smile
at your innocence and skill, for all this while.
I found 'your precious gift' on the stairs,
where with a friend I sat.
Perhaps, you saw or decided not to see,
for I did smile and do all that.
Anyway, I hope now you know,
my eyes follow you everywhere you go.

> —*From the delegate who wants to be forgiven*

I didn't have to look for the messenger; she was already standing nearby, waiting to transfer the message of love. God bless her soul!

She giggled again. Was our poetic chit-chat so amusing?

'It's a girl's thing; they giggle at anything and everything,' my adjacent partner (I still don't know his name) spoke up for the third time as if replying to my unannounced question. He was psychic, I am sure!

'I hope she finds all this as amusing as the messenger does,' I whispered to him.

'She will; she's beautiful,' he said. A streak of jealousy overpowered me suddenly. I didn't respond to my partner (I don't even want to know his name now).

'Excuse me, your note,' said the same girl, coming to me again, after five hour-like minutes. I quickly took the note from her.

Chit No. 4
She to Me

Oh delegate of Gabon,
I honestly did not notice,
even if your eyes were following me.
But I am glad we are having the poetic word,
At lunch, did you try the yoghurt? (I told you, I suck at rhyme).

—From Ishita (friends call me Ishi)

A 240-watt smile quickly lit my face. Yoghurt is called curd in India; anyway, I could call it yoghurt, curd-yog, damn anything, if she wanted so. I quickly looked in her direction. I wanted to excuse myself and go out and shout, 'The most beautiful girl in the committee has just flirted with me; okay, if not flirted but kind of flirted, for sure. Else she wouldn't have replied to my chit. All that my mind registered was that she didn't mind.'

Engulfed in nerve-wracking excitement, I began to write down the next chit.

Chit No. 5
Me to She

Ishi or Ishita, am I your friend? Please let me know,
Last time I questioned, your reply cheesed (forced) me to go.
Cheese is sweet, I want you to understand,
Probably you haven't yet tried out Aaryan's brand.
I am humble, I don't boast,
For breakfast I had French toast (see, your poetry inspires me).

    —*From Aaryan (my friends call me Aaryan only, yaar).*

The messenger threw a wide smile after going through this chit, reassuring me that it definitely was the best of the lot.

Chit No. 6
She to Me

Aaryan,
I like making friends; I think I just made one.
This poetic interaction was definitely fun.
Enters a cool breeze,
requesting me to endorse Indian cheese.
The MUN is more than political power play,
isn't Karan Johar (the Bollywood film director) almost gay?
(I am genuinely running out of words now).

    —*Ishi*

Mom must have prayed for me back in Chandigarh today morning, for I felt blessed. My apprehensions and doubts about the flirt were all washed away by the sea of emotions the last chit generated. She endorsed Indian cheese; she liked me... Ahaaan...she liked, I liked, we all liked.

I had to flirt back with something very catchy yet subtle; something funny but not hilarious; something...

'We adjourn,' the Director's voice pierced through my thought process, transforming the most important something into nothing. The last one hour had passed away so quickly.

'Damn it. Why can't they have longer sessions?' I grumbled softly, as everyone got up in response to the Director's last words.

I did not get up though. It was a part of the plan; it was her time to walk her walk to remember, for me.

She got up. She searched. She saw me still sitting. She started to walk towards me. She was near my table. She was right next to me. Was she so into me?

'Hi,' it was her.

'Hey,' I got up as the protocols of chivalry dictated.

'Thanks again for keeping the book,' she said, obviously expecting me to hand it over.

'Here,' I said living up to her expectations.

'Thanks again,' she said.

'Well...'

Before I could continue, a loud voice boomed through the speakers again 'Delegates, please leave.' It was the Director, damn it, now that it's clear who the villains of my love story were.

We quickly moved out. Three people flocked down the stairs again this time—she, me and the silence.

Walking next to her was enough for my tongue to freeze and vocal chords to face premature retirement.

'Sometimes...,' she began.

'Sorry?' God, she must be thinking I wasn't paying attention to her while the truth was that I was so lost in her that I didn't care to listen what she spoke.

'Friendship *mein* no sorry and thank you,' she said suddenly in her accented Hindi, uplifting me and the atmosphere to a lighter level.

'You love Bollywood, don't you?' That was all I could manage, after losing my short-lived chit-chat confidence.

'Mom loved Bollywood, when Dad was away to Saudi for work...She used to have a date with the Khans and the Bachchans every Friday in Singapore, that is...' she stopped speaking.

'And what about your dates?'

'What about me?' she asked confused.

'What did you do every Friday evening?' I asked the most important question.

'Nothing much, hung out with friends and stuff,' she replied casually.

'Does stuff include your boyfriend as well?' I asked carefully, wondering for how long my Mom could have prayed!

'I don't have a boyfriend...'

'Me neither,' I said.

She laughed, I laughed, problem solved.

❦

Some two minutes later, outside the garden of India Habitat Centre.

'So I'll see you tomorrow,' she said. The crowd was thinning and the cars were ready to go back. I panicked, 'No wait!' As I said, I literally panicked. 'I study in B.N. World School.' Fuck, serious fuck, was this all that my mind could come up with in extreme situations? Aaryan, the player, had lost all his flair.

'Okay,' she said politely, confused at how my behaviour was symbolic of the Sensex, the regular ups and downs.

'So, I'll see you tomorrow,' she said again, after I had asked her about her school, her friends and even the weather in Singapore.

My mind was still making up ideas to stall her, when a

shout was heard.

'There you are!' It was Boza—Boza my best friend, Boza my saviour, Boza the princess, Boza the rescuer, all in all. Hail Boza!

'Hi, Ishita, right?' she asked immediately before turning to me, 'Aaryan. You can't get lamer than this. Everyone is waiting in the car and why the hell are you not picking up your phone...I had to walk all the way from the parking lot...' she huffed. 'Couldn't even tell Chloe that I have a cell phone.'

Boza, my friend, just called me lame; Boza, my best friend, just highlighted my flaw—of not turning the phone on general mode once the meeting ended. Boza, my friend, said it all in front of Ishita. All slay Boza!

'Hey, I am sorry, I didn't get your name,' Ishita tapped Boza from behind, after the latter had finished with her accusations and warnings and orders and what not (no doubt, I am exaggerating).

'Oh, I am so sorry,' Boza turned and shook her hand 'I am...'

'She is Boozie,' I cut her, 'it's payback, bitch.'

'He means Boza,' Boza said politely, eyeing me with contradictory expressions.

'Okay, I think I need to move now. I don't even know where my teacher or teammates are and our bus leaves soon for the international students' hostel,' Ishita said.

'I'll walk you till the parking,' I offered.

'And me?' Boza asked playfully—B.I.T.C.H., I cursed within.

'You can walk me,' I said.

We all laughed.

'So what grade are you in, Ishita?' Boza questioned her as we walked towards the parking area.

'I am doing IBDP, first year,' she said, adding as an afterthought.

'By the way, IBDP is?'

'International Baccalaureate Diploma Programme,' I finished her sentence, supplementing the full form.

IBDP, equivalent to Class XII, CBSE, ISC, SSC, HSC, was an international level, pre-university, two-year course, which most international schools in India and around the world followed. Basically it meant, 'No Boards studying with the help of laptops and international recognition'—a convenient coincidence that we both were studying the same course.

'You people too!' Ishita exclaimed.

'Yeah, we too. We have so much in common, nah,' I said, beginning with the flirts again.

'Not really,' Ishita said and laughed at foiling my attempt. Boza laughed at seeing it fail; I laughed at myself.

'I just remembered, I…I had an urgent call to make,' Boza suddenly said and excused herself, leaving the two of us walking slowly as she dashed to the parking lot.

'So it's just now you and me,' I started again.

'Aaryan, stop flirting!' Ishita said in a voice which sounded like it wanted just the opposite.

'Didn't I do that way back?' I asked innocently.

'Yeah, yeah, way back is like one minute ago, isn't it?' she said sarcastically.

'Okay, I am sorry. No more flirting,' I said.

'Thank you.'

'For today,' I added.

She laughed either at the sentence or at me. I laughed for she laughed and then we reached our destination, the parking lot.

'That's my ride,' she said, pointing towards an almost-loaded blue bus.

'That seems to be a nice ride. Wonder where is mine!' I said.

'Okay, till we meet again, bye,' she said and started walking towards her bus.

'Hey, Ishi,' I shouted.

She turned around, 'Enjoy the ride,' I said, she smiled and turned away.

'Hey Aaryan,' I heard Boza's voice from behind. 'There is another ride back to school—a real bumpy one.'

She laughed, I laughed, problem solved.

🐎

Back in School
Dinner

'There you go, Aaryan,' Chimmy said, keeping a pile of books on the dinner table.

'From rookie to booky,' announced Karan, as everyone sitting on the dinner table laughed.

'Is this for me?' I questioned Chimmy, unaware of what was happening.

'It'd better be; it took me an hour after Boza's call to extort these from the juniors on my dorm floor, but *The Notebook* is mine though,' Chimmy said.

'Notebook? I thought these were novels,' Batra said timidly.

Wait a second, *The Notebook*, the phone call, the novel, Nicholas Sparks—it all began to make sense all of a sudden.

'Oh Chimmy, thanks a ton,' Boza shouted from a distance, juggling with three dinner trays.

'I love you, Boozie,' I said, pulling out a chair for her.

'So, now you can actually start a normal conversation with her,' she said.

'What is happening here?' Karan voiced everyone's question.

'Aaryan, why did you need the books...I mean novels?' Chimmy asked.

'And who is this *her*?' This time it was Batra.

'Hang on everyone,' I requested and picked up a glass to slowly start drinking water. Phew! There was so much to share, yet so little to tell.

We had returned rather late and I hadn't got the opportunity to tell everyone together or anyone singularly about *the someone*.

'Aaryan dude, curiosity kills,' Karan snatched the glass from my hand, after a patient wait of two full minutes.

'God, you were having water as if it was whiskey,' Boza commented.

'Huh, sorry...so, yes the story,' I said, wiping my face with my hand.

'So everyone, I have something to tell you guys,' I said, enjoying their curiosity.

'Aaryan yaar, cut the crap,' Batra said impatiently.

'Okay, Batra, I am sorry. So you all know that I was out of school today,' I paused and took a bite of the rice and manchurian.

'Aaryan, don't irritate them now,' Boza said, taking the spoon from my hand for the second time in the day.

'Hey, let me eat. I am hungry,' I protested.

'So are we—about your story, about what happened at the MUN,' Chimmy said, while Karan and Batra shook their heads in unison.

'Fine, so I met this really cute girl.'

'Five minutes for dinner to end,' the speaker came to life again and so did the memories of the day.

☙

That night in the hostel
'So you will seriously stay awake for the night and read the...I

can't remember,' said Karan.

'*A Walk to Remember,*' I said as I changed into my boxers. We were in our personal paradise.

'Karan, let's bet for Sunday tuck,' Batra suddenly spoke up from his bed.

'Two hours at the maximum,' he placed his bet.

'I say three,' Karan said.

'And if I am up for more than that, I get all of the tuck,' I said, already thinking of what to do with their share.

'Okay, done,' Karan said, getting into his bed.

'Do you people mind if the lights remain switched on?' I asked for the sake of formality, of course.

'We won't, but the Assistant House Parent would if he decides to come up for a random check,' Batra said.

'He won't. He only decides to raid our rooms when his supply of porn, chocolates and gum gets finished,' Karan said.

We all talked for some time more till we heard the speaker come to life for the last time in the day, 'Lights off, sleep well and be well.'

※

Some three hours later

'So how far have you reached?' asked Karan in a groggy voice after he had finished his daily dose of dope.

'Ummm...second chapter.'

'Ha, you slept in between, so you lost the bet. Sunday tuck...aaha,' he suddenly got excited.

'I mean second chapter of the second book, buddy.'

'But how did you manage?' he asked. His eyes told me he needed sleep. I made a mental note of discussing this with Boza.

'Well, the book is kind of interesting...romantic...much

better than *Playboy* atleast,' I said and we both laughed.

'Aaryan has fallen in love, *pyaar*, and Aaryan will not sleep and say goodbye to every star,' Karan said and crashed on his bed, dropping into deep slumber.

I kept on remembering what my adjacent partner had said the last afternoon 'There were still two days and a lot of chits to pass.'

🜚

The next morning

'Did you dope last night?' queried Boza over our especially arranged early breakfast.

Shazia and Kabir were sitting in one corner of the dining hall while Chloe sat on the parallel table, sipping hot (yes, she's hot) coffee. A tube-tank top and a tight-fit pair of jeans—she was a symbol of why Paris is called the fashion capital of the world.

'Get me some more coffee, please,' I said, after gulping down the remains of the fourth cup.

'Look at your eyes; they look so Karanish,' Boza said, eyeing me. Pun was intended.

'My eyes are red, because last night I didn't use the bed,' I rhymed, giving shape and colour to her wild imagination. 'Get me some coffee please...here, take my wallet too.'

She took the wallet even though we were sitting in a paid, school-owned cafeteria (this explains why we are *besharam* best friends).

Three books, their three love stories, one author, one me, one she, one my love story and my eyelids shut. Sleep is deadly and love is lethal. The combination is so powerful that it leaves you helpless, forcing you to sleep later (like now).

'Aaryan, move, everyone has left,' Boza said, shaking me

vigorously after, I had no clue, how long.

'But Mom, I don't want to go to school till I get Ishita,' I said playfully.

'Oh shut up,' said Boza, now shaking me real hard. 'Aaryan, are you seriously high?' Boza asked, looking concerned.

'A sleepless night is a lover's right,' I said smiling. Perhaps I was high—high on romantic novels; high on caffeine—maybe, four cups is something after all; high on the most dangerous drug—yes, the drug which is so passionate that it leaves the person confused, and so strong that it leaves you weak in the heart.

7

He Lives, Likes, Loves, Loves Some More

Time is relative—I am not the first glorified soul to suggest this, Einstein had done it first. This simple conclusion found origin in the patient waiting in the car. I felt stuck and the world was stuck in a traffic jam.

'We will get late,' I said, looking at my watch in desperation.

'It's 7.58 a.m. The meeting begins at 8.40. What's the worry?' Kabir asked.

'But,' I revolted, 'I have to meet someone, I mean, some delegate.'

'*Bhaiya*, how far are we?' Boza asked the driver.

'I can see the damn building. We are at the most 200 metres away,' I shouted.

'Aaryan, stop shouting.' It was Chloe ma'am, instead of Boza, who probably just ignored my anxiety-injected pangs.

'Sorry,' I said turning back to look at Boza. She smiled in acceptance.

'That's it. It has been twenty minutes and we haven't moved at all,' I said, after two minutes of patient waiting.

No one reacted. 'Okay, I am,' said I, quickly opening the door and getting down. I didn't need to complete the sentence with 'walking down'.

'Get back in, Aaryan!' Chloe ordered me. Fuck, Chloe ma'am, there will be a hundred more opportunities to show the authority you demand but fail to command.

'Ma'am, please,' I begged. 'I will meet you there.'

What was the reaction? I don't know, for my action was walking away, anyway.

The walk to remember (yes, yet again)
8.11 a.m.
Running through a traffic jam, all suited and booted. God, I feel wet. Oh, its just sweat.

8.14 a. m.
> *I enter the complex and see her bus standing there.*
> *God just answered my silent prayer.*
> *Fuck, I am so charged and hot,*
> *and I look terrible; at a bathroom, I need to stop.*

8.17 a. m.
> *I find a washroom on my way.*
> *I splash some water, set my hair.*
> *Liberally use the paper roll*
> *on a high toll.*

Some seconds later
> *My mouth feels dry,*
> *No time to waste.*
> *Water from the toilet tap, I gladly taste.*

8.19 a. m.
> *I reach the ground, ease my pace.*

I look all around for that pretty face.

8.22 a. m.
I stand alone in a secluded corner,
Suddenly somebody taps me from behind.
'Hi', I hear an angel say.
Startled, I stutter, stammer and say,
'Hi', still it's my lucky day.

'So what were you doing here, standing all alone?' Ishita asked.

'I was umm…nothing. What are you doing here?'

'Well, I saw you standing here all by yourself, looking out for someone.'

'Oh, I was just exploring,' I covered up.

'Exploring?' she seemed confused. '

And searching,' I added.

'For?' she asked.

I took a deep breath and said in a joking tone, 'if I say it was you, what would you think?' Ironically this was so true.

'I would think or rather presume you are a chronic flirt,' she said and started to laugh.

'Does that work in my favour?' I asked her saucily.

'Well it does, unless you believe this is a dream.'

'Oh, don't talk of dreams,' I said stifling a yawn.

'Not slept well?' she inquired.

'Not really. I was reading,' I said. With her, truth came out instantly.

'On the issue of women empowerment in war-stricken countries?'

Was this the topic to be discussed today? I thought.

'I wish,' I smiled, 'I was reading novels.'

'So what's your genre?' she asked interestedly. I silently

thanked Boza for giving me an opportunity to excite (I mean, interest) her.

'Well, I prefer romance, Eric Segal and...oh, yes Nicholas Sparks,' I added quickly.

'I knew the answer this time,' she said and smiled.

'You did? How?'

'Destiny.'

Damn it, she could get seriously vague and mysteriously deep at times. We walked together to the committee room. We were surprised when we reached there—those who gave the stare, I mean our esteemed jury or Chair, were absent themselves. Around forty children sat in the room in comparison to the eighty-odd that were supposed to be there.

'Must be stuck in the jam,' I suggested.

'Jam?' she was confused.

'There's a massive one outside, just near the lights,' I said, thinking, 'I will have to clear all your doubts and myths, my mystical princess.'

'Hey,' my princess suddenly greeted another guy, who had just walked up to us. His physical appearance made me look like Prince Charming, so I gave no thought to any competition.

'This is Rohit, delegate of UK,' she introduced.

'Hey, Aaryan, Gabon,' I said plainly.

'Oh yes, the concerned delegate,' Rohit said.

He laughed, she laughed, sadly I forced a laugh.

My cell phone started buzzing. 'Excuse me,' I said as I picked up the call.

'Oh, hi Boza! Yes I am safe. I know I shouldn't have...yeah (in a hushed voice) I met her...(moving away from her). She is looking so hot. Yes, I know everyone is late...please, Chloe *ka jugaad pa*. Oh boozie (loudly) *jugaad pa* means take care of her...okay, bye!'

'What does *jugaad pa* mean?' Ishita asked me as I approached them again.

'Was I that loud?' I asked sheepishly. Wait a minute, could she have heard *everything*?

'Well, it's Punjabi,' I said, not exactly wanting to tell her what *jugaad* really meant.

'Mum's Punjabi,' she said a little slowly. 'But you are…'

'Palathingal?' she cut me. I nodded while the other guy, knowing he wasn't needed anymore, excused himself politely. 'My Dad's Christian.'

'Love marriage?' I asked.

'Yeah,' she replied, looking away.

'Cool yaar…so you want me to teach you Punjabi?' You can surprise your Mom when you go back,' I offered.

'I wish,' she said very slowly.

'What?' There was something about her which was hidden and deep.

'So what is the fee?' she asked suddenly.

'Let me see. For this tedious task, I think a cup of coffee at The All American Diner outside should be fine,' I said, giving a crooked smile.

You are such a FLIRT,' she said as I ducked her feeble punch.

'So kudiye, Punjabi class on?'

'Yes sir… *ji*.' She added the *ji*.

'By the way, to whom were you explaining the meaning of *jugaad* on the phone?' she asked again.

'Boza,' I replied.

'Oh, where is she? She wasn't with you before either.' So she was observing me.

'She just reached with my team some time back,' I told her.

'Then how come you are here?' she asked, surprised.

'I came for you,' I said slowly.

'Aaryan, don't joke. It isn't funny all the time,' she said in a serious, dark tone.

'Do you see me laughing?' I asked her, trying to induce some brightness.

'Aaryan...you...I mean...it's just that you don't know anything...and...'

'Delegates, sorry for the delay. Please be seated quickly. We will begin with the present delegates as of now,' the Director's voice broke the pause. When had he entered? Why he entered, I don't know. All I knew for sure was that the villain had arrived.

☙

And what? And why? And how? And never before has an 'and' ever haunted my mind so badly. It had been almost eternity since the meeting had begun and both my partners in crime still hadn't reached. Trying a new messenger could prove risky. God, I needed Boza now.

'Yes, delegate of Gabon,' the Director said, recognizing me with my raised placard.

'Can the delegate please be excused?' I asked.

'It is called a point of personal privilege,' he stated mechanically.

Damn the UN rules! 'Isn't going to the washroom more of a personal necessity than a privilege?' I questioned with pretentious innocence.

A few heads turned and one of it was hers—mission complete.

'Delegate, please leave,' the Director said just the right words!

I got up and quickly walked down the aisle with the chit about the 'and' in hand. She sat in the first row, left corner. Can you guess why I decided to untie and then tie my shoelace just when I stood parallel to where she was seated?

She looked at me briefly. She did just when I kept the chit on the floor and got up to move again. 'Yes,' I congratulated myself as I saw her bending down to probably pick up an accidentally dropped pen, just before I closed the door.

୨୫

I found a new chit resting on the same spot on returning some time later. Some delegates had arrived, with the ongoing commotion camouflaging my bending to pick up the chit. I almost ran back to my seat, wanting to know where the 'and' ended. All I got in reply was a word which itself in the English language had no significance. The word was 'nothing'.

This is not going the right way. I tore another page from the notepad again and began to carefully write.

> *Ishi (ta)*
>
> *I don't flirt, I won't flirt. I just wanted to hang out with you, you know. I mean, I know you know. See, this doesn't even make sense and so does your getting angry; and if you think I have crossed the LoC (language of control), I will make sure it doesn't happen again. Slap me the next time I flirt. Okay?*
>
> *P.S. Now you will again think that I am flirting but blue really suits you.*
>
> *—A 'sad' Aaryan*

I had to pass the chit again. 'So, women in Iraq,' the Iraqi delegate began to explain when the Director cut him short, 'delegate of Gabon, why are you playing "plane crash" with your placard?'

So you can recognize me, you idiot. 'So that the esteemed

Chair could recognize the Delegate,' I replied coolly.

'Is it so urgent? Anyway, to what point do you rise?' he apparently hated me and I so loved that.

'To the point of personal privilege,' I said.

'But you just went,' he reasoned.

'I wish I had control.' This time most of the committee laughed.

'Delegates, please maintain decorum. Please leave, delegate,' the Director said. He simply wanted to get rid of me.

I quickly got up, walked down the aisle and this time accidentally, of course, my hand brushed against her country's miniature flag and it fell down!

'Oh, I am so sorry,' I smiled to Ishita, as she also bent down to pick it. I thrust the chit in her hand and walked out a happy man.

I re-entered the room after five minutes, looked at her and followed her look. Her reply was kept on the edge of the table. I walked down the aisle, quickly picking up the small piece of paper.

Aaryan

Fine! Get ready to be slapped, for you won't change...your shoelace is still open. Your girfriend's flirting, isn't that how the proverb goes?

P.S. You are the seventh guy to compliment me on my attire, so I take it as a compliment.

—Ishi(ta)

My heart beat increased with each word I read. So she had checked me out...well, literally from head to toe. Did she indirectly want to know my relationship status? Well girl, I am open, single, ready to mingle and then do jingle, jingle. I began to write the reply.

Ishi(ta)
Well. I don't have a girlfriend. You see, I am a different guy.
Guys like me don't find acceptance in the Indian society. I
don't know about Singapore but not many guys here believe
in true love and meaningful relationships. I hope you are
smiling and happy and hey, I am not gay.

—Aaryan

My self-obsession resurfaced once I read my reply again. It was just perfect...well almost! 'How do I pass you the chit, Ishita?' I slowly questioned myself.

As my mind bubbled with ineffective ideas followed by a sinking heart at the realization of the same, my eyes graced me with a vision—a vision that found abandoned on the floor a rubber band. Thus an almost perfect idea originated in an almost perfect brain.

In India, Bollywood is religion and since kindergarten my ears had been drilled with the saying 'preach what you practise'.

I picked up the rubber band, stretched and twisted it in the shape of a launcher, entangled the chit in the loop and after saying a silent prayer, launched the chit in her direction.

Distance, speed and time (no, this isn't an ode to Physics) were going to decide my fate.

Distance: The chit covered the required distance.

Speed: It was quicker than I thought.

Time: It hardly took any.

Accordingly all was perfect...well, almost, as the chit found a station, in fact superseding my expectations and Ishita's to land at the Director.

'My apologies for the interruption, delegate of Russia,' the Director interrupted the speaker. 'I have apparently been hit with a small piece of paper which in its contents reveals a very interesting fact about someone named Aaryan.' He paused deliberately to gauge the effect on the audience.

'Yes, delegates, I'd like to share a little joke. Mr Aaryan here is happy, but not gay.' Hoots of laughter emerged from all corners of the room. I sank down in my chair as he continued, 'And this chit is addressed to a certain Miss Ishita.'

G...r...e...a...t! The jerk had to involve her as well. Down sank my chance to dance.

'Without wasting the precious time of the committee, I would request Aaryan and Ishita to please get out. I suspend them for the day. Thank you.'

There was pin-drop silence in the room. Even though no one knew my name there (we were always addressed as delegates), and presuming that it wouldn't make sense for the Director to start looking into each delegate's id-card, I raised my placard.

'Yes, delegate of Gabon, does the washroom wait again?' the Director asked as everyone laughed.

'No sir, I am Aaryan,' I said bravely.

'Oh!' Even from the distance I could see him sneer. 'Then leave,' he said sternly as the laughter and murmur subsided to silence. I shoved the paperwork into my bag and started to walk down the aisle.

'And who is Ishita?' the Director suddenly asked. I looked in her direction, only to find a girl sitting expressionless with water-filled eyes. I had screwed her chance as well. She wouldn't have expected this, travelling all the way from Singapore to be in the conference and then get suspended from it.

'Please, Director, she has no role in this,' I pleaded in a weak tone.

'Who is Ishita?' the Director asked again. Ishita suddenly got up and stood with her head bowed.

'Oh, right under the eye,' remarked the Director, faking surprise laced in sarcasm. Now you know why he is the villain of our story.

'I am sorry,' is all that Ishita could murmur. She gathered her paperwork and moved to leave the room; seconds later I followed her.

❦

'Hey Ishita...Ishi, wait,' my frantic call echoed through the painfully peaceful corridor. She ignored it and kept on walking. I followed her past the room where the ECOSOC meeting was taking place. Boza was inside, sitting peacefully while her best friend was calling out the name of the girl he had started to like and now was about to lose.

Now I needed Boza, the friend who had always helped, who knew how to tackle such catastrophes involving a girl and me.

My clouds of thoughts cleared to give way to the storm of reality as I saw Ishita reach the end of the longer-than-long corridor and turn left towards the stairs, to leave the first floor and my view.

'Ishi...ta...,' my prolonged call boomed and so did the marble floor in the rapid action of my feet. I caught up with her midway on the staircase. 'Ishita, listen,' I said, holding her hand from behind.

Silence and then a glare; I left her hand and fell in step with her. 'Ishita,' I repeated but she gave me the I-don't-care stare. We finally reached the reception area. The middle-aged receptionist was either seriously busy, or seriously trying to act busy.

'Ishi...'

'Enough, Aaryan, I haven't come all the way from Singapore

to get suspended during the conference. You...you just don't know anything. My teacher will screw me when she gets to know this!' her voice conveyed her conviction mixed with her angst.

I stood there transfixed; angels are supposed to repulse anger. She started walking towards the glass door. In an impulsive stroke, I dashed towards her, but in a decisive stroke she decided to press the breaks and halt abruptly. She tried her best to warn me as she pressed her vocal horn, 'Aa...r...yan!' but my slippery, formal shoes decided to skid along the marble floor and the result...

Thought for the day: if you run into closed glass doors, your fall is inevitable and so is the pain!

☃

Never before had a fall given me such a high; never before had my eye been so close to her eye; never before had my throbbing head been cushioned in such a comforting lap; never before had the pain brought along such gain.

'Hey Aaryan, are you alright?' she asked, caressing my forehead.

I marginally opened my eyes. 'Where am I?' I said and smiled.

'My filmi hero,' she said and slapped me playfully.

'Listen Ishita, I am really...,' her hand covered my mouth as she completed the sentence for me, '...sorry'.

She inched her face forward; I followed suit and SPLASH! A violent sprinkle of water on my face and all my dreams and hopes were watered down. I opened my eyes and adjusted my frames only to see two monsters and a beauty standing around.

'He's coming around,' I heard the beauty speak and then extend her hand for me to get up. I held out my hand dreamily, a little tipsy by the fall. Was I still dreaming or had she suddenly grown manly with rough hands?

'Okay, now get up slowly,' I heard a deep manly voice instruct me. I tightened my grip around his hand and with his pull and my push, I managed to get up.

'Thanks man,' I said, rediscovering my senses.

'Its okay, but why are you people out of your committee room?' the man asked.

'Actually...we were suspended,' the hurt in Ishita's voice hurt me.

'Oh...anyway, if you need first-aid or anything, we have set up a medical room right next to The All American Diner in the lawns,' he informed us, opened the door and left.

'You better sit for some time,' the receptionist advised, indicating towards the sofas in the left corner.

'Yes, my head is umm...still like getting hammered by something,' I said and the receptionist gave me a confused look.

'I'll get some water to drink,' the other guy offered and walked towards the reception counter.

'Who was the other guy?' I asked Ishita, once we were seated on the sofa.

'Conference staff, the member of the organizing committee of the host school,' she replied.

'Listen Ishita,' I said massaging my forehead with one hand, 'I am very sorry. I know I took it a little too far with the chit-passing,' I added, giving the puppy-eye expression again.

'It's okay, but you still didn't need to run like a mad bull... so, even I am sorry. Perhaps, I overreacted,' she said and smiled. I smiled back. 'So it's a fair square,' she said, holding out her hand.

'Totally,' I said, finally getting the chance to embrace it all.

'So how was the fall?' she asked me teasingly.

'Well umm....it was like falling in love,' I smiled crookedly.

'Stop flirting now at least.'

'Am I?' I asked.

'Well, not really, because you know what Aaryan?'

'What?' I asked eagerly.

'You never fall in love; you fly in it.'

She smiled, I smiled, problem solved.

❧

Call it Cupid's conspiracy or a convenient coincidence, neither of us could find our respective teachers outside. So ultimately, after some serious searching, Ishita suggested that we go to The All American Diner to kill time till lunch and I agreed wholeheartedly.

'Sir, ma'am,' the waiter gave us the menu and left.

We started going through the menu in silence. One look at the price list, a depressing realization hit me hard, rendering all my plans, aspirations and our future together go down the drain.

'So what will you have?' I asked Ishita politely.

'Hmm...cold coffee or something. You tell.'

'Me?' I started coughing to camouflage my real intentions. As my left hand covered my mouth, its counterpart began the destined search.

'Are you alright?' Ishita stroked my back while my heart sank to find that both the pockets of my coat were empty. I started coughing with more force.

'Hey, we need some water here!' she said aloud to the waiter. In the meantime, I fished again in my pockets. The waiter returned with a mineral-water bottle. Fuck! I had seen the price on the menu a few seconds ago; the fucking bottle was worth a hundred bucks.

The forced, artificial coughing had left me honestly gasping for breath. Ishita quickly opened the bottle and filled my glass. I drained it in one go.

'Better?' she asked in such a cute manner that I was ready to suffer a sore throat for the rest of my life.

'Yeah!' I said, wiping my face and loosening my tie.

'Listen, if you are not feeling well, we can go to the medical room outside.' Her eyes revealed genuine concern.

I smiled internally as the plan was almost at the pinnacle of success.

'And then we can find our teachers too,' she suggested, as we were getting up.

'Hell, no...,' I sat down instinctively again.

'What happened?' she asked, looking confused.

'I...I think, I am fine now...let's order,' I said timidly.

'Are you sure?' she asked again.

No, my wallet is with my best friend and this place is damn expensive! 'Yes, I am sure,' I said.

So here I was, sitting with the most beautiful girl in an upscale eating joint, penniless and hopefully hopeless.

The waiter came and took our order. 'Two glasses of cold coffee with whipped cream, chocolate sauce and ice cream,' she said. 'Is everything okay?' Ishita caught me mentally calculating the bill.

'Yeah...yeah...actually...no.' It was her eyes and the way she looked at me. It was so difficult to lie, to defy the power of truth.

'I think I left my wallet with Boza,' I said softly.

She kept quiet for two minutes...two long minutes and then finally spoke, 'Did you devise this all so that I could treat you for returning my book or is this the Punjabi class fee?' she said seriously. A second passed and we both burst out laughing.

It took a two-hundred-rupee glass of cold coffee to finally stop her laughter. The best part was that she was paying.

'So, which song would you dedicate to me, if you had to?'

she asked, taking a sip from her cold coffee.

I grinned sheepishly when she fired the question as it totally caught me off guard. The way the hazel blue eyes stared at me made me wonder if any hidden romantic agenda was on the cards.

'I don't know. It will probably be something unplugged—you know from my heart to your heart,' the flirt game was on. 'So when are you going back to Singapore?' I added after a few seconds, as her vocals seemed to have gone on a silent mode.

'I think it'll be, when you say nothing at all,' she said, softly addressing her own question and ignoring mine.

Oh yes, so she did get the catch, Mr Wit-hit. She was leading 2-1 and I was happily being led. She just kept looking straight into my eyes, silently. Baby you win at my cost, I thought!

'What makes you happy? The fact that you so cleverly extracted your farewell treat from me or is it that you won't get subjected to Ishitaism after tomorrow?' she asked.

Pop! The bubble was burst by a pin named reality. She was going back tomorrow and we would probably never meet again.

'Excuse me, I'll be back in a jiffy,' she said as she looked in the direction of the washroom. 'Be ready with an answer that bowls me out...' Her momentary touch on my shoulder during her last statement made me mutter to myself, 'girl, you sure did bowl me out.'

I was still dreaming or to be more precise, fantasizing, when she returned.

'Still thinking of an answer,' she commented as she caught me in the act.

'Err...ummm...no; it's just that you are going tomorrow.'

'You already occupy a place in my virtual world, I mean Facebook, MSN and all, silly,' she said with her trademark cuteness and the gloomy look that had graced my face seconds ago suddenly turned into a glorious smile.

'And we have our whole life ahead. We are just seventeen and not to forget, Singapore is a nice country to holiday in,' I replied hopefully.

'I think we should finish this quickly and find our teachers.' She surprised me again with her abrupt, uncomforting tone.

Silently she kept looking down as I emptied my glass, sniffing in coffee and something more.

'The meeting should be finished by now,' Ishita remarked as soon as I kept the empty glass on the table. I checked my watch which seemed to second what she had said.

'So, let's go out and meet our respective teachers and teammates and tell them...' I paused, 'that we got suspended,' I ended bravely.

'Aaryan, you make it sound like we just got caught making out or something,' she said casually. We both burst out laughing again. She signalled to the waiter for the cheque and then came another pile of embarrassment.

'Sir,' the waiter came and placed the bill in front of me, looking at me expectantly.

I uneasily flinched in my chair, thinking whether I should stab myself with the unused butter knife kept on the table.

And then, Ishita did something which not only erased the embarrassment but also made my day even more special. She kicked me under the table. She tilted her head a little and performed a little dance with her eyes...they were indicating towards something in her hand. Something green...oh, the cash.

I grinned like an idiot.

Her eyebrows contracted, signalling the urgency. I took the money from her hand under the table and confidently placed my hand on the table, beginning to count the money, after a quick glance at the bill.

'Keep the change,' I said in Bollywood style as we both got up and moved out. The ground was again at its noisy and social best. All the delegates were busy chatting in groups and eating food.

'Your acting is getting better by the hour,' Ishita said as she momentarily held my arm.

'It's all credited to a girl named...'

'Ishitaaa...!'

No, I had not taken her name. It was a feminine shriek... *her teacher*!

'Good afternoon, ma'am,' she stammered. Her teacher took the few steps that separated us.

'This is a boy, I mean this boy is Aaryan. He is also in my committee.' Okay, so this was my introduction.

Her South Indian teacher eyed me like a lady eyes the rotten vegetables in the *sabzi mandi*. Her grey-streaked hair, large figure and angry eyes made it all the more easier for me to feel intimidated.

'*Namaste*, ma'am,' my voice trailed my eyes, which were continuously going towards her big bosom. She had a sudden change of expression which made her look like a female jailor.

'Okay, I will see you around then,' I said and excused myself with my eyes searching for Boza. I found her near the food counter, standing with some unknown guy and flashing her rare girlie smile.

'Hello, boozie baby,' I tapped her shoulder.

She turned around and suddenly began, 'There you are. Why the hell do you have a cell phone if you can't pick it up?' Boza, who was acting all coy and feminine (for the boy, obviously), suddenly came in her tom-boy avatar again. 'By the way, this is Arpit,' she said, softening again. Bloody chameleon!

'Hey,' I greeted the guy, 'Umm...Arpit, if you don't mind,

can I take Boza aside for two minutes?'

Both of them were surprised—Arpit out of a word called 'jealousy' and Boza at me for knowingly screwing her chance.

'Sure,' he faked an artificial smile. Boza smiled to him apologetically as I caught her hand, took her aside and told her everything.

'What on Earth did you do? Pinch some girl's ass or something?' Boza said loudly. We both looked at Arpit, who looked at us with the same expression—shock!

'Softly yaar, I just did what you told me to do,' I said, resting my hands on her shoulders.

'Take these hands off,' Boza said and looked again towards him.

'I'll see you around...later,' he said and left.

Boza's temperature rose, so did her blood pressure and vocal volume, 'I told you to get suspended? Aaryan, you know, if the headmaster comes to know, he will eat me alive.'

'Easy Boza. Easy, okay! He won't come to know, Baba. Who will tell him? Not you, for sure,' I said softly, as a few passersby stopped to enjoy the free show. Luckily the curtain fell with Boza's next reply relatively subdued.

'I won't tell anyone...but, did you meet Chloe ma'am?'

I just shook my head and shrugged my shoulders in reply.

'Well, obviously, dog, you are so lucky. I met Kabir, he had our lunch coupons. He told me that Chloe has gone to meet someone in Delhi. She won't be back until late evening.'

'Hey, that's great. So, now I can take Ishita out till your next meeting ends,' I said excitedly.

'You can, what?'

'Yaar, we are suspended for the day, so we can't obviously attend the next meeting. That means we are free for the next three hours,' I informed.

'So?' Boza demanded.

'So...so, since Chloe is also not there, we can just go out and see some sights.'

'Hmmm...is she fine with it?' Boza asked curiously.

'Should be yaar! Haven't asked her till now, though. I left her with her teacher outside the Diner...I'll go and find her later.'

'I see...so, you went to the Diner?' she asked another question.

'Yeah...'

'But your wallet is with me,' Boza spoke just the words I was about to speak.

'Yes and she had to pay...so, please return my wallet. I don't want to go to Delhi all *bhooka-nanga*,' I said and laughed.

'But are you sure she is going to agree?' she seemed doubtful.

'I'll just check with her then. Have you had lunch?' I asked quickly. I had to ask Ishita out fast.

'Actually I was waiting for you...,' she paused for a second and cleared her throat. 'But, I think you already have plans.'

'Yes, I hope...give me the wallet.' I, true to my idiot character, ignored her hurt over the situation and went on.

She took out the wallet from her skirt pocket and handed it over to me.

'Thank you,' I replied to my best friend, who was now rubbing her eye. 'What happened?' I asked quickly.

'Nothing...nothing some dust particle or something...you go now. Lunch is going to end,' she smiled feebly, hugged me goodbye and left.

I started walking around the ground in search of Ishita. I saw her standing with one of our committee guys.

'Hello,' she waved to me, as I approached her. The guy turned around, saw me and excused himself.

'So what did your teacher say?' was the first question I asked her.

'Nothing,' she replied. 'Nothing?' I queried.

'You know what, it is strange, but for the first time in my life I am actually doing stuff which I shouldn't be doing,' she said.

'Like?' I asked.

'Like getting suspended, having coffee with a guy whom I hardly know and even paying for him (that hurt me) and not telling my teacher or my teammates that I got suspended,' she smiled mischievously.

'You haven't? Well, anyway, do you want to add something more to your newfound rebel side?' I cleverly laid the trap.

'Hmmm...like what?' she seemed to be falling in it.

'Like going out and sightseeing in Delhi...'

'Are you crazy?'

'No, that's why I am asking you to come along. It will be fun...a day in Delhi. Your last day in India, c'mon,' I said in the best possible persuasive voice.

'I know, it's pretty strange actually...coming to India all the way and yet not seeing anything except this place and that crappy hotel,' she said, falling into the trap.

'Exactly, you have spent so much money to come to India for this dumb conference and then going back without even seeing the city. Imagine what will your friends say?'

'Hmmm...I haven't really bought any gift for my friends till now and we have to go back tomorrow evening...But what about my teacher?'

'Where is she?' I asked.

'Having lunch, maybe,' she replied.

'Fine, then let's move right away,' I said and held her hand. Surprisingly, not once did she try to withdraw her hand.

8

He Lives, Likes, Loves, Loses

'Pinch me, please!' Ishita shouted, trying to outdo the noisy engine of the CNG auto. I obeyed her gladly, not letting go of any chance to touch her smooth skin.

'Ouch...I didn't mean it seriously,' she pinched me back. I smiled, enjoying the pain.

'This is the first time I am sitting in an Indian auto,' she shouted again. The auto-driver scowled. The traffic outside was at its best and so was the noise inside the auto.

'Easy!' I signalled to her with one hand, while the other was used to conceal my laughter.

Ishita adjusted herself (her skirt actually) and came close to whisper in my ear, 'This auto has a lot of benefits.'

'Like what?' I asked, unintentionally placing my hand in such a way that it touched her semi-naked leg.

'The benefit is that...it vibrates,' she said and we both started laughing loudly.

'Oh my God, I can't believe I just said it...or the fact that I am doing all this,' she said, amidst peels of laughter.

Phut! Phut! Our auto came to a sudden halt; apparently three cows had decided to sunbathe on the road.

We both got down and straightened our formal attire. '*Paaji, kitne huye*,' (how much is it?) Ishita asked the driver in her broken Punjabi. The driver surprised by a not-so-Punjabi-looking, skirt-and-shirt-wearing girl speaking in accented Punjabi, did not react. I repeated the same statement.

'*Challi* (forty),' he said almost instantly.

I turned around and gave a poker-faced smile to Ishita, who stood there open mouthed. 'Not fair...,' she said softly. A group of school-going students, who were passing by, suddenly stopped to look at us and stare.

'Boooo,' Ishita turned around suddenly to the youngest kid in the group. We both started laughing and the visibly petrified child with the rest of the group began to walk again rather briskly.

'Let's walk down...but before that, I want a picture with this historic auto first.'

'Sure,' I smiled. So as the vehicles honked, cows relaxed and drivers mouthed angry expletives, a suit-wearing boy and a formal-skirt-wearing girl posed merrily for pictures on a busy Delhi road for an illegal cell phone's camera.

❦

We got in the rickshaw we had found after walking for some hundred metres.

'Central Secretariat Metro station,' Ishita announced the name of our destination apprehensively to this new auto.

'Yes, I thought or rather I know for a fact that you haven't travelled by the Metro rail. You see, I want you to remember this day...,' I paused, 'and me.'

She smiled and took out her wallet to pay.

'Allow me, lady,' I said like a French connoisseur.

'But you paid for the first auto...one and the same thing,'

she argued like a French freak.

'Ishitaaa...*atithi devo bhawo*—Guest is God,' I said, taking her wallet and keeping it in my coat pocket, while I paid from my wallet.

We quickly climbed the stairs and entered the Metro station.

'Holy cow, it has already been twenty minutes...' Ishita exclaimed after looking at the digital clock near the ticket counter.

'I know, just two hours and forty minutes now. So, for which station should I buy the ticket?' I asked her, as we joined the queue at the ticket counter.

'You are supposed to be the local here, not me,' she said intelligently.

'Hmmm,' my tube-light brain produced a 1000-watt idea this time. 'Do me a favour; can you go and buy some water from that shop? I am so thirsty...here take the wallet,' I gave her my wallet.

Two minutes later came my turn to buy the ticket. 'Till where?' the ticker seller asked in a bored tone.

'Well...till where does this Metro go,' I said like a fool.

'Huh...till which station do you want to go, bhai?' he asked with the irritation all government employees are famous for.

'Till the last station and back,' I said. He eyed me from head to toe, as though I looked like a well-dressed terrorist. He gave me the tokens and I paid him from Ishita's wallet (I didn't have a choice).

'There you go,' Ishita gave me the mineral water bottle and my wallet.

'Oh...thank God,' I opened the lid and drained half of the bottle. 'You want some?' I asked Ishita, after wiping my lips and loosening my tie.

'Actually I do...but you have already put your mouth to

the bottle,' she reminded me.

I smirked, 'Have it...maybe the water might taste better now.' I couldn't really judge, if a blush crept on her or was it due to the Delhi heat.

We passed through the token verifying terminal next. The Metro was about to leave the platform. 'Quick,' I said, grabbing her hand. We entered the train and banged into an old, serious-looking uncle who gave us the stare of our life just as the electronic door shut. We both suppressed the urge to laugh.

The Metro started to move with a little jerk, which was enough to make Ishita fall on me and me fall on that old uncle again. Even as the uncle stared and swore, Ishita tapped him on his shoulder to ask, 'Uncle, I know we aren't making it any easier for you after your hectic office, but I just wanted to let you know that I like your tie.' Believe it or not, the grimace on his face turned into a short smile and my sweet, little, innocent, smile-spreading angel turned to me.

❦

'Aaryan...Aaryan wake up; we have reached,' Ishita shook me.

I groaned and murmured something that sounded like 'Karan shut up.'

'Get up Aaryan...' Ishita shook me a little harder this time and I opened my eyes only to find her hair falling in them...I thought it was still a dream...

'Aaryan! Get the fuck up,' my angel spoke like the distant cousin of the devil and I got up with a start.

'Huh...wha...,' I raised my head and saw Ishita's face. 'Good morning, Ishita.' I opened my eyes fully wide.

'Hi!'

I looked around. We were sitting on the back seat of a stationary radio cab which we had taken from Connaught Place after shopping, eating and clicking some more pictures. 'Since how long have I been sleeping?' I asked.

'Umm...the entire ride back,' she said and laughed. The fact that I hadn't slept the previous night was more than clear now. I rubbed my eyes again and saw my reflection in the rear-view mirror. A crushed coat, a displaced tie, a messed-up hairstyle—all seemed like an after effect of a make-out session.

The taxi driver handed us an on-the-spot printed bill. We paid him (from my wallet) and got out. 'Here, let me carry these,' I offered as Ishita was carrying two small, little polythene bags. She had bought bangles and *Phulkari duppatas* and other knick-knacks for her friends.

'Na...they are not heavy. But what do I tell my teacher? I mean if she sees me walking in with these bags, she would get suspicious.'

'Hmm...You left your bag with your friend, right?' I asked her and she nodded. 'I'll keep them inside my coat till then,' I offered and she agreed. Just as I thrust the polythene bags inside my coat, my hand brushed upon something that was already resting wrapped inside the inner pocket. Oops the gift—I had sneaked out from the shop where Ishita was shopping to the jeweller's shop next door and bought a gift for her. I had thought of giving her the gift once we were in the taxi but fatigue took over and my plan flopped...that brought me to another point.

'Hey Ishita...Umm...why didn't you move my head away from your shoulder...after I had slept?' I know I had asked a foolish question.

'Actually I did...four times to be precise, but you seemed to take an anti-clock direction and come back to my shoulder after every two minutes.'

I looked at her embarrassed. 'Sorry yaar, I didn't mean to...I mean I wasn't being touchy or anything.' I wanted to make her understand I was caring, not crass.

'Dude, had I felt uncomfortable, believe me, I would have punched you right in your scrotum.' I stopped walking, shocked. 'Alright...maybe not...but the point is you looked so cute sleeping that I didn't want to disturb you.'

A smile instantly lit up my face—a smile which had nothing to do with her physical beauty; a smile which had nothing to do with her unpredictable yet mature behaviour; a smile which had nothing to do with the day we had spent together but *a smile which had everything to do with the thing called 'love'*!

❀

'I am in love,' I whispered into Boza's ear. We were sitting in the CRV, heading back to school.

'Good for you then,' she hissed back. I grinned for no apparent reason...in fact, I had been grinning ever since I had walked Ishita to her bus and sat inside the CRV.

Chloe ma'am seemed to have noticed this. 'You seem to have had a wonderful day, Aaryan.'

I blushed like a newly wed bride. Kabir, who was seated in the front, turned around and saw me. 'Yes ma'am, Aaryan definitely seems to be enjoying...the MUN, I mean.'

His attempt at sarcasm had no effect on me. A strange excitement made me nudge Boza again, 'I am in love.'

She gave no reaction. I pestered her again, 'I am in love boozie...seriously, I am in love.'

She just snapped at me with her look. I sunk back in my seat, wondering what was wrong with her. Boza had been acting funny ever since I had returned from my wonderful date. Whatever I had narrated to her, her standard response had been, 'Nice! Nice!' I looked again towards Boza, but she turned her face away to look through the window.

'Whatever,' I murmured and diverted all my attention to the song and the reason for the music in my heart—Ishita.

༠ৡ

'What the hell is wrong with you?' I asked Boza. We were walking towards the hostel. From the path we had taken, Boza's dorm was to come first. It was 7.25 p.m. and everyone was in the academic area engrossed in their studies. '*Boza Korbi,*' I shouted and held her from behind, stopping her in the action.

She took a deep breath and turned around, 'Aaryan listen, I'm tired. Okay?' she said, taking off her stilettos and holding them in her hand, as if to give authenticity to her (in)valid reason.

'What's wrong with you, Boza? Listen, if you are angry that I didn't get anything for you, I am sorry, yaar. I was so low on cash...the gift was expensive, yaar,' I said, knowing very well that I had committed one of the biggest blunders of my life.

Scandalized, she opened her mouth to speak and then stopped. She repeated the same action twice and then finally just said four words, 'Fuck off, you womanizer.' She turned around and started to walk briskly.

The last two words stung me; honestly they did. I mean 'fuck off' was a pleasant way to address, which we people use more than 'please' and 'thank you', but 'womanizer'? Me? I started to follow her at her pace.

'How dare you call me that?' I gave a medium shout, controlling my anger. The campus police (security) was the last thing I wanted then.

'Because you are one...I know I am your best friend...but still Aaryan, it's just been a month with Rhea and before her Roza, Shalini, Priyanka, Prerna and the American bitch, Natalia. Wow, six girlfriends in a year!' she clapped with her hands to disgrace me further.

'Whatever, but you still can't term what I feel for Ishita as lust...I truly care for her, damn it. She makes me feel... different,' my voice trailed off. 'I didn't even try to kiss her today. Do you know that?' My vision turned hazy for a minute. It took a tear to clear it.

Boza walked up to me and asked me to sit down on the raised pavement. 'I am sorry, Aaryan. I just overreacted, I think. But you don't get the main fact correct—she lives in Singapore. You know it better than me that you aren't exactly what I can call an emotionally balanced person...she will go away and then what? Don't say Facebook and Skype. I just want you to be happy and to be very honest...,' she paused and wiped a fresh tear with her hand. 'I don't think she is serious about this.'

The anger quotient inside me rose to the height of Everest. I got up, fighting back my tears, 'YOU...YOU are jealous, Boza... just plain jealous,' I said and started walking towards my dorm, leaving her sitting on the pavement...*alone and lonely*!

༈

Dear God,

I know I don't talk to you often. I know I don't talk to Mom and Dad either, even though they go out of their way to avoid the same thing from happening. I know I haven't been the best human being around. I haven't valued relationships; I haven't been the ideal son to Dad; I haven't reciprocated the love I feel but don't express to Mom. I know I am not exactly what you may define as a friend. I know I live an escapist's life, which to others is a reason of envy and to me is a reason of failure. To the people here, I am one of the most popular boys but I know how lonely and insecure I feel within me. I know it's been five years since I came

*here and honestly, I don't regret it either. But still, I know I
am wrong somewhere. I know I have continuously hurt the
people who care for me, like Boza today, but even she should
understand, God...*

*Ishita is different. What I feel for her is different; what
I want us to be is very different from whatever my past has
been. The fact that I will see her tomorrow for the last time
perhaps...till I don't find a way to meet her, is already mentally
ruining me. Please help me God! Mom says, 'You are there
and you answer all our prayers!' Today all I ask of you is
to make it work for Ishita and me and Boza and everybody
around me. Please, I know I seem to know it all, yet I feel
I am incapable. Please.*

—Aaryan

I opened the register, tore the page and folded it before keeping
it in the drawer of my cupboard, where ten odd letters rested
in peace.

⁂

Thak! Thak! Thak!

'Mmm...,' I groaned.

A louder knock followed.

'Who the fuck is it?' Karan shouted in a groggy tone, while
I flipped my pillow on my head.

A fiercer, louder and harder bang came this time. I got up
and switched on the light. It was 5.30 a.m. We three (Karan,
Batra and I) had chatted till 3 a.m. in the morning. I had tried
my best to sleep before they both could gang up and extort the
details of the day from me, but all my efforts had proved futile.

Skipping dinner had only resulted in a stomach ache. The

other eye-opener had come from Karan when he had informed me that even Boza had skipped dinner. Chimmy had said that she had heard Boza crying in the toilet.

So, after smoking four cigarettes with Karan (one for tension, one for pain, one for loss and one for gain), I had begun narrating my Delhi *yatra* with Ishita followed by the little 'edited' conflict with Boza. Even Batra, who was now not in the room (he jogged every morning with the juniors) had for the first time stayed up till 3 a.m., listening to my tale of friendship and love. I had somehow managed to fall asleep at 4 a.m. only to be forced awake by the loud and continuous banging on the door.

I opened the door. A visibly frightened junior stood there. 'What the fuck is your problem?' I asked him bossily.

'I...I came to give this to you, Aaryan *bhaiya*,' he said, pointing towards a suit zipped and packed in a coat-hanger.

'Who sent it?' I asked, rubbing my eyes as a big yawn escaped from me. As far as I knew, I hadn't asked anyone for the suit.

'I don't know, *bhaiya*. I am getting late for the morning games. If sir sees me, I will be detained. Please take this...' he said, holding out the suit to me.

I took it from him and just as I was about to bang the door shut, he spoke, 'I am very sorry, *bhaiya*, but I forgot to give this also.' With scared eyes, he held out a small piece of paper.

'Okay...go now, quickly,' I ordered and slammed the door shut.

'So, what do we have here?' Karan asked, looking up from his bed. I walked up to his bed and handed him the suit. He unzipped the zipper of the suit cover.

'Dude, it's an Armani.' My face mirrored his expression of shock.

'Read the note,' Karan spotted the piece of paper in my

hand. I pulled my study chair and began to read it quickly.

My dear Gummy Bear, Aaryan,

Before beginning I want to clear certain things:

1. This is not an apology letter.

2. I still believe that you are a_____ (fill in the blank, according your conscience).

3. I did not attend dinner; because I was tired and nothing else.

Now Mr Aaryan, just fit your butt in this suit for it took me one dangerous hour after 'lights off' to sneak out to that loser, Riteish's dorm. I had to flirt with him for some dreaded thirty minutes to get this. So, if I see you wearing something else, be prepared to get assaulted.

And yes, I still hate, dislike, disagree with you about yesterday. Do come for breakfast at seven. It's your last day with her; enjoy it in style. All the best and I hate you.

Your unfortunate best friend,

Boza

A large grin broke on my face as I finished reading the letter. 'Whose is it?' Karan asked eagerly.

'My best friend's,' I replied, relieved.

❧

'Somebody is going to charm the ladies today,' Chloe ma'am commented as I entered the cafeteria for our early breakfast. Kabir choked on his coffee while Shazia smiled politely in appreciation. But where was my main critic?

'Sorry, I am late,' I got my answer after two minutes. She came and took the seat next to me. 'Nice suit, Aaryan. From where did you get it?' she asked him in her characteristic manner.

'Somebody very close to my heart got it delivered to my room today morning. Do you know who it can be?' I asked her seriously.

'Well, if that somebody special is looking hot today, then I might know that person...'

'Oh hell! Yeah, that somebody special is looking smoking hot today.'

I laughed, she laughed, problem solved.

❧

I opened the small little box again and closed it. Batra had covered it with some of his artsy wrapping sheet the previous night.

'Stop playing with it,' Boza shouted at me.

We were sitting in the grounds of IHC, waiting for my angel. The first and the last meeting of the day was to begin in another ten minutes and there was to be tea, followed by the closing ceremony. Ultimately would come the part I didn't want to even think about, leave aside writing it—the 'end'.

I started playing with the box again. Boza snatched it from my hand this time. Before I could take it back, I heard a male voice. It was someone from Boza's committee.

'Hey Boza, aren't you coming for the meeting?' a tall and muscular guy asked her.

'Hey Rishabh, I am,' she replied.

'I'll walk you then,' he suggested. No, don't take my best friend away. I will be left alone and waiting. 'No, I am waiting for someone; for a friend.' If your best friend calls the girl you like her friend, then it is definitely heartwarming.

'Okay, I'll sit with you until then,' he said, pulling up a chair.

'Sure,' Boza said out of partial courtesy and partial boredom, 'and, by the way, this is Aaryan.'

'Aaryan.'

'Rishabh.'

We shook hands. 'Nice suit, man,' he said and Boza winked at me.

'Did I miss something?' he asked, feeling left out. 'No...no, it's a hostel thing,' I explained.

'Okay,' he said and started talking with Boza, while my eyes, my face, my heart, all turned towards the entrance.

'I think we should move now,' Rishabh said, after ten minutes had passed. The meeting was going to start in two minutes flat.

'Okay,' I looked towards the entrance one last time, sighed and moved a reluctant frame.

※

The rapporteur was taking the roll call when I reached the committee room. Apart from the casual stare from here and there and a sneer from the Chair, no one seemed to glorify my suspension.

Our seating arrangement had been changed today, for Gabon (my country) was placed in the sixth row. I still didn't have a clue to where France was going to sit today.

The rapporteur reached the alphabet 'F'.

'Delegate of Finland.'

'Present.'

Next was France, but she wasn't there or was she...

'Delegate of France.'

'Present and voting,' I heard her reply and instantly turned around to check the geographical location of such a biologically and mentally uplifting voice.

I was unable to spot her in the roughly fifteen rows behind

me. 'Delegate of Gabon,' the rapporteur announced.

'Present and voting,' it took me a lot of strength to mouth the two words normally. I turned back again to find her.

In vain,

in pain.

I sat for a minute when I suddenly got an idea. I opened the chit pad and wrote a formal MUN chit, just to see if she would reply or not. She would...please pray for me.

Delegate of France,

Which resolution are you supporting?

—*Delegate of Gabon*

I folded the chit and signalled to the messenger. Ten minutes passed, no reply. Ten more minutes passed, yet no reply. Perhaps the messenger has forgotten to give her the chit, I thought. So I wrote another chit to her after five minutes. Again, no reply. I tore another chit frantically and this time, while handing the chit to the messenger, asked him, 'Are you delivering the chits to the correct delegate?'

I hoped he would say 'no', but not all wishes come true. He nodded in the positive and took my third chit. I still foolishly waited for a reply. After another five minutes passed, all hopes began to diminish. I took out the small box from my pocket, opened it, looked at it briefly and closed it again.

Dejected,

defeated,

disillusioned,

devoid of help and hope...

I sat still waiting for the most miserable meeting of my life to end and some questions to be answered.

'I formally proclaim the 2008 DPMUN shut,' the Director banged the hammer and the whole room broke into an applause. Everyone got up with a smile, except me. I turned around and started scanning the rows behind.

I finally found her standing in a group with some other delegates. My steps automatically took me in her direction.

'Hey man, sorry about yesterday. Find me on Facebook. I am Dhananjay,' the Hungary guy (my adjacent partner) stopped me on the way.

'Sure,' I replied hurriedly and moved on.

A group of delegates blocked the aisle for their group photo session. One of the girls, with whom I had had a brief conversation the first day, drew me into the picture, 'One with the suspended hottie,' she shouted and everyone hooted while I tried to maintain courtesy.

It took me three more pictures and five times more of 'excuse me' to break from the group and head towards the spot where I had seen her earlier...only to find the French flag, an empty chair and the door at the south end of the room open.

❧

'Hey, how did it go? Where's Ishita?' Boza ran up to me and asked excitedly on seeing me standing at her committee room's door. I just hugged her tightly, trying to fight back the liquid from my eyes waiting to burst for Ishita.

'Hey Aaryan, is everything okay?' Boza asked. I broke the embrace and wiped my eyes.

'Let's walk,' her warm hand pulled me along as I began to narrate the last three most dreadful hours of my life. 'Let's go and find her now,' Boza said, after I walked out of the washroom on the ground floor.

'Yes.' I held Boza's hand again and we walked out of the

reception area into the open lawns.

Boza, who seemed to have made a lot of friends in the past three days smiled, shouted out, 'Goodbye! I'll be back in a moment. Yes, I am on Facebook!' to many people.

After walking a short distance, she pointed to a group standing near the tea counter, 'There she is.' Ishita stood among a group, sipping tea and laughing merrily. I felt as if I didn't even exist in her world. I started walking towards her, but Boza stopped me midway.

'Not in the group. Leave her alone. Till then, let's go and meet the others.' It took me some amount of persuasion to act rationally, but Boza insisted.

☙

'I just don't get it. I mean, I just don't...,' I said and rested my head on Boza's shoulder.

We were sitting on the 'historic stairs'. She stroked my hair in a motherly fashion. 'I wish I had such silky hair, Aaryan,' she suddenly said and despite the situation, a momentary smile crept on my face.

'There you are,' Chloe ma'am and Shazia walked up to us, followed by Kabir. 'Aaryan, you look terrible. Is everything okay?' Chloe asked, as she drew closer.

'Yes ma'am, he is just going through an anxiety pang. He thinks he might win something today,' Boza lied for me with conviction. Kabir sneered.

'Don't worry, Aaryan. If you have given your best with a clean heart, then God will reward you,' Chloe gave her characteristic reply to every situation.

Suddenly the loudspeakers began to blare, asking everyone to assemble in the auditorium for the prize distribution.

'C'mon everyone,' Chloe said and I blinked my eyes hard

to expunge the liquid they had collected.

'Let's move people,' I said enthusiastically, while everyone laughed, Boza smiled, understanding the real cause of my motivation.

'Aaryan, enough! She must be somewhere around, okay?' Boza assured me, as we made our way through the auditorium.

'It's not that, Boozie; it's our last day together and she is acting like this, especially after yesterday. I...I...,' I stopped at the I.

Boza gave me an I-told-you-so look. Just as we were about to enter the auditorium, a feminine voice called out my name. I turned around instantly.

'Hey, are you Aaryan?' a short girl came up to me and questioned.

'Yes,' I replied apprehensively while Boza stood there, plainly curious.

'I am Ishita's friend,' she huffed in between. The excitement seed in me went through another round of germination.

'Where is she?' the plant had already started to sprout.

'In the Diner; I have it all covered up for her. Go quickly,' she said and left.

I looked at Boza expectantly and the excitement tree looked all green and healthy. 'Yes, go Aaryan. I'll take care and say you are in the loo; some last-minute nervous release,' she winked and I side-hugged her before running in the Diner's direction, leaving my best friend behind.

☙

An avalanche of emotions and frozen eyes accompanied my jog till the Diner. I stopped at the door to steal a quick glance at my reflection in the glass door. Reassured at my parents' physically flattering genetic combinations, I opened that glass door and scanned all around. I found her sitting and then...*the same boy* walked up to *the same girl* who was sitting on *the same table* on which *the same order* was already placed. He pulled out a chair and sat down. Everything seemed to be the same except for the deathly *silence*.

Sometimes silence becomes the most excruciating sound; sometimes the mind becomes a musical symphony of clouded thoughts, questions and clarifications but the vocals fail to present the sound of a conversation.

'Aaryan,' she said slowly, after some time.

'Hmm...,' I tried my best to find my voice.

'Aaryan, listen, I just wanted to tell you that...'

'Why did you ignore me today?' I prepared myself physically and emotionally to question.

'I...I...I don't have an answer,' she said, avoiding my eye.

'Ishita, look at me and answer,' I said bravely.

'I don't want to clarify, Aaryan,' her voice was getting weaker with each sentence.

'You don't have a choice,' I said as my voice grew bolder.

She tried to take a sip of her cold coffee, but her shaking hands gave away her nervousness. She kept the glass back on the table.

'I avoided you today because I think, I...I...don't know,' she changed her statement at the last moment.

A thunderous storm raged inside me and a streak of lightening struck, 'This is lame, Ishita...it's like, I just can't decipher your emotions. You behaved so differently yesterday; you were so warm and nice, and I thought you and I could...,' I stopped midway.

'Could?' her voice was nothing more than a whisper.

I took out the small box from my pocket, reached out for her hand, opened her palm and placed it on it. 'This is for you,'

I said each word with emotion.

She took a deep breath and kept the box on the table without opening it. 'You want to know why I avoided you, don't you?'

'Yes,' I said.

'Well, Aaryan, I avoided you today because I think I have started liking you.'

Did the last line make any sense? Perhaps no, but then, ancient scriptures say that love defies all reason and logic.

'I don't understand Ishita...you like me, yet you avoid me?'

'I don't believe in relationships,' she said in a sudden matter-of-fact tone.

'Do you believe in your friends and family?' I asked in exasperation.

'Friendship is a relative term and family...I haven't really experienced what it feels like to be in one,' her voice trailed off on a note of bitterness. A tear escaped her eye and that burned my eye.

'What makes you say that, Ishita?' I asked her slowly.

'My parents are divorced,' she whispered and closed her eyes to prevent any further liquid salt to slip.

I had lived in a hostel for five years and I knew how it felt to be away from one's family, but I still had one for consolation. Ishita had none. I reached out for her hand again and squeezed it.

'My parents,' Ishita began again in a very low voice as I adjusted my chair for better reception. 'My parents were high-school sweethearts—that's what Granny told me. They were totally into each other and got married. Then I was born.' She took a sip from the cold coffee as I sat there, holding her hand and listening. 'Everything was fine till Dad's company transferred him to Saudi Arabia for work.'

'Then what happened?' I asked cautiously.

'Dad was having an affair and Mom found out. She took to

drinking and then there were fights, custodial battles and finally Dad was able to prove that a drunkard woman could not take care of her daughter in an alien country.' Another tear dropped from her eye and she wiped it away quickly.

'So, where does your Mom stay? In Singapore only or...?' I questioned.

Ishita smiled very feebly, 'Mom? I wish she was alive,' she said each word through a torrent of tears.

Everything suddenly made sense but I didn't know what to do next.

'So you see, I just don't believe in the concept of getting into it relationship. Mom and Dad did when they were in school and this is where it led them.'

'Ishita, I know love is a very heavy word, but I want to take on the burden. I mean, I want this to happen and I swear we will make this work. Screw the distance...please,' I pleaded.

'After a long time Aaryan, I felt different with someone. The first time I saw you struggling with the model, something inside me ordered me to help you out...and I am glad all this happened. I will always remember you, Aaryan. I will always remember the last three days. I am sorry,' she said, wiping her face with the napkin kept on the table.

What was happening—the first girl in my life whom I had liked and wanted to love also liked me but couldn't love me? It's all *karma*, I think. Rhea's sad face haunted me momentarily.

'Ishita...please,' my eyes too had turned moist.

Before she could reply, her friend dashed in and came straight to our table. 'Ishita, quick, Subo is getting mad. We have to leave now...' Ishita got up immediately.

I sat there transfixed, unable to gauge what was happening or what was about to happen. A feeble 'wait' was all that I could muster through my vocal chord. Ishita unzipped her bag and took out something.

'I want you to keep this; it was my mother's...her memory for me. Now it's mine for you. Take care, Aaryan, I will miss you,' she said and turned away, leaving behind moist eyes, a small box, a book and a boy who had lived, liked, loved and loved some more only to lose everything over a period of three days.

9

He Lives, Likes, Loves, Loses, Learns

The first week without her.

Monday

'Aaryan, get up, it is 7.15 a.m. Breakfast will end soon and you haven't had anything since last evening,' Karan shook me.

I tried to reply but my voice failed me. Yesterday Boza had found a boy sitting in the Diner, all alone, lifeless with coagulated dreams, staring at a book. The night for him somehow subsided but not his pain. Even now, his every breath hurt, every blink burned, every heart beat bled.

Karan and Batra exchanged concerned looks. 'Aaryan, if you want to skip school, why don't you go to the medical centre? There's no point staying in the dorm, man,' Batra said.

'C'mon Aaryan, it's Monday...she definitely can't be more important than chocolate waffles. Just fuck her.' Karan said casually, but it lit a serious rage in me.

'FUCK YOU', I said angrily and marched off to the medical centre.

Tuesday

'How is Aaryan now?' Chimmy questioned Boza, Karan and Batra. They all had bunked some lecture and come down to the editorial room.

'I went to give his night-suit and toiletries yesterday. He was sleeping at that time actually, but the nurse told me he had low blood pressure,' Karan informed.

'I really cannot believe it. Aaryan, of all the people, is doing all this for a girl; a guy who has the reputation of going through girls as quick as dirty laundry,' Batra said, as Boza and Chimmy shot him a disgusted look. He apologized, looking embarrassed.

Boza, who had been silent till now, suddenly spoke, 'I logged in through his account on Facebook just to check if she had left some message or anything.'

'Has she?' Chimmy asked eagerly.

'Nope,' Boza sighed.

'Hey...why don't we call her this Sunday? I mean I can call home and get them to call her. It'll be a local call for my Dad,' Karan suggested.

'That's a great idea, Karan, only if Aaryan had her number,' Boza winced.

'Oh...didn't she give it? Anyway, Boza, did you try talking to her?' Chimmy questioned.

'Tried...she declined my friend request; no reply to the e-mail; heartless bitch!' Boza said with emotion.

'Hmm...how about adding her friend on the Facebook and then explaining the situation to her?' Batra suggested.

'Tried that too, Batra. Don't tell it to Aaryan; the reply wasn't the least encouraging. I swear I don't know what mess Aaryan has got himself into.'

'I think it's worth it. Aaryan showed me her pictures...she

is hot, man,' Karan said.

'Fuck you!' was all he got in reply from everyone.

Wednesday

I showered in the medical centre, got discharged and went for breakfast directly. I spotted Karan and shot him a faint smile. He smiled back reassuringly. I guess this is what friendship is... forgiving the fucks!

Thursday

Early morning

'Oh, you scared me,' Batra exclaimed, after he switched on the light and found me sitting on my bed, staring intently into the laptop.

I smiled and a yawn escaped my mouth.

'Hmmm...since when are you awake?' Batra asked wearing his jogging shoes. It was 5 a.m.

'Quite a while,' I closed my laptop screen and rubbed my eyes.

'Hmmm...completing assignments?' he asked sceptically.

'Not really; I was just seeing our pictures together... And Facebook, to check her reply,' I said and yawned loudly.

'I wish I could get some sleep, somehow.'

Evening

'Prep begins,' the speakers boomed and I opened my Maths book. It was high time I gave a little consideration to the subject. Mid-terms were just two months away and I had to give up the practice of staring into the Maths book and seeing Ishita's face. I tried to concentrate and do something.

Thirty minutes and two exercises down, I looked up from

my book, only to find Boza staring at me.

'What?' I whispered to her.

'Nothing...' she smiled in a weird way! Confusing, these girls can be, I swear.

Night

Night...there is something very mysterious about it. The darkness of the sky, the glory of the moon, the fabled beauty of the stars—their flickering light, a bright second of hope, a dull moment of despair. There is definitely something romantic about this time of the day. Celebration for some; for others, it announces the end of the day, its misery, pain and experiences.

For me this night reminded me of her; it reminded me of my failure. She still hadn't replied to my e-mail. It reminded me of my temporary smile. It reminded me of the cigarettes I had smoked, of my parents and Boza, who would be unhappy if they came to know about this. It reminded me of my inability to get over her, to live and laugh normally with my friends. It reminded me of my insomnia; it reminded me of sleep.

Friday

Economics

'So what is the theory of scarcity in Economics?' Mrs Iyer, our forty-year-old Economics teacher shouted, with her big butts facing the class and face turned towards the white board. The hands shot up as usual.

She turned around and scanned the whole class silently and finally said, 'Aaryan.'

'Y...e...s...' my head lifted itself in reflex.

'What do you think scarcity is?'

'Scarcity...Hmm, lack of something.'

'That's vague...can you elaborate?'

I looked around for help. Karan who was sitting next to me nudged me under the table.

'Scarcity is the lack of the basic necessities in life,' I said, trying to recollect the lame definition.

'So what are the necessities of your life?'

'Ishita,' I said slowly without thinking.

'What was that?' she demanded.

'Booze, boobs and basketball,' Karan whispered and I looked at him for a moment.

'Aaryan...is everything alright?' she asked.

'Yes, it's food, shelter and...,' a yawn interrupted me and then I said 'clothing'.

'Factually correct, but for you I think it is sleep and detention,' she smirked. I sat down...looking blank.

2nd Period

Psychology

I don't remember anything; I was sleeping on the last desk... anyway.

3rd & 4th Periods

English

Romeo and Juliet, Ms Stella, my favourite teacher, wrote on the white board. Everybody groaned in unison. 'For once, the class seems to respond pretty quickly,' she joked. She wrote something in big bold letters—LOVE. 'Okay, since most of you don't have your books today, we will play a game today. It's simple. Everyone just has to say the first thing that comes to their mind after thinking about the word. I'll begin, okay? For me love is love,' she said and everyone laughed. 'C'mon, let's begin with you, Ritwik.'

    Ritwik: 'Love is complicated.'

    'Hmm...is it?' Ma'am asked.

    Mandeep: 'Love is happiness.'

    'It surely is.'

    Chimmy: 'Love is acceptance.'

    'That's deep.'

    Rhea: 'Love, I don't believe in it anymore.'

    'Treat every encounter like therapy.'

    Batra: 'Love is being accepted.'

    'Doesn't that correlate with Chimmy's description?'

    Boza: 'Love is friendship.'

    'That's debatable.'

    Aaryan: 'Love is best left unsaid.'

    'Hmm...'

5th Period

Maths

Dear Students

    I am busy with the headmaster. Please revise the quadratic equations.

                                         —*Mr P. Pandey*

Karan read out loudly from the small piece of paper, the peon had brought in class. I got up to go to the students' locker and get my laptop. I had thought of taking it to the washroom and lock myself in the cubicle and look at pictures transferred from my illegal cell, again.

    'Where to?' Boza asked, on seeing me get up and walk towards the door.

    'Umm...the school office,' I lied and that too without feeling bad or guilty. What's happening to me?

6th Period

Accounting and Business

I quickly swiped my entry card and the class door opened.

'Welcome, Mr Aaryan,' welcomed Mr Frederick Uranus Caver Kentucky, the proud headmaster of B.N. World School for the past twenty years.

'Good morning, sir,' I stammered.

Mr F.u.c.k was a retired Army colonel, stern, swift in body and word, with a six-foot frame, booming voice, and broad shoulders. The worst part was he recognized me well, mostly for my evil deeds. The last encounter was when he had caught me bunking.

'So, young man, what is the reason for coming fifteen minutes late?' he demanded.

I couldn't possibly tell him that I had snoozed off in the toilet cubicle while looking at her pictures. 'I was in the toilet, sir,' I refined the truth.

'But I was told you had gone to the office,' he said and I looked at Boza.

'Yes...after the office, I went to the toilet,' I said slowly.

'Did you not hear the speakers or the bell?' he asked.

'I did, but...I was disposing off the waste,' I said innocently as a giggle engulfed the class.

'Well Mr Aaryan, it's been a while since you visited me in my room.'

'Yes, sir.'

'March off to my office right away!' he said, reliving his army days and walked out. I walked back to my seat to collect my books and bag...and it was then that Boza gave me a cold stare.

7th and 8th Periods

Alone with the headmaster in his room—need I say more?

Lunch

'Hey man, just heard that you got screwed by the headmaster,' said Kshitij, the school captain walked up to me and said.

I gave a plain smile in reply.

'And yes...about this beard, I don't know if the "Devdas" look is in or not, but it really won't work with the school authorities or me,' he said diabolically.

'Devdas?' Boza quizzed, after he walked off to find more people to slay.

'Devdas was a lover boy who never got his love,' Avantika, who had decided to share our table, joked, but the sad part was that none of us laughed.

The weekend

Ishita still hasn't replied,
my tears haven't dried.
During breakfast

'Hey Karan, are you going to call your parents?'

'I don't want to but I have to...they haven't refilled my account,' he replied.

'Okay, I will come along,' I said after two seconds and Boza choked on her bite.

I slapped her back while Karan offered her water. She was wearing a sports bra today, I think. Boza understood my growing intention and quickly backed off, flashing a welcome-back-my-sick-friend smile. I had been acting 'positive' in her language since the last evening.

With my beard shaved off, no mention of Ishita and a smile, I had actually enjoyed dinner and the school screened movie last night. So I was acting like a hormonal pig again after a week.

We got up and went towards the phone booth. Luckily, there wasn't a long queue. After five minutes of patient waiting, my turn came.

'Hello...umm...may I talk with...is that Mom?'

'Aa...r...y...a...n,' Mom gasped. Mothers and melodrama go hand in hand.

'Hi! Good morning.'

'Morning son, how are y...'

'Eeeeeeeeeeeeeeeeeee,' I heard a loud shriek from her side. The second female in my house had snatched the phone from the first female.

'Aaryan...are you okay?' Ritika asked.

'Yes. Why?' I asked cautiously.

'Because you have called only after bloody ten days despite possessing a fucking mobile... Yes, Mom...no swearing! Okay, sorry Mom!' she said into the phone.

'Where's Dad?'

'Already left.'

'Okay, tell him...actually don't say anything. Hand over the phone to Mom,' I said in a polite tone.

'I have no value in this house...wait till I get married,' I heard her dying voice as she handed the receiver to Mom.

'Aaryan *beta*, call more frequently and sometimes try to reply to my e-mails and messages. It feels nice to hear your voice,' she said emotionally.

'Yes, I have just been busy, Ma,' I lied to the woman who knew me more than myself.

'I understand,' she assured me and accepted all that I didn't want to share.

Suddenly my voice started to break and my vision became hazy. I heard Boza shout out something in Tibetan in the adjacent phone booth.

'Umm...Mom,' I cleared my voice and spoke.

'Is everything alright?' she asked me instantly. Intuition and mothers go a long way.

'Yes...yes...actually Mom, can we pray together? Please,' I whispered.

She seemed silent at first and then smiled into the phone. I closed my eyes and prayed on the phone with Mom for a life full of love.

10

He Lives, Likes, Loves, Loses, Learns Some More

Four Sundays later…

A Walk to Remember—the proof of her existence in my life—
the book she had left with me. It had been thirty days, seven
twenty hours, forty-three thousand two hundred minutes and
some million bleeding seconds since she had disappeared from
my life and reappeared in my dreams every night. The book
had ever since rested peacefully in the drawer for I couldn't
muster the courage to open it, to run my fingers through
the pages which once her fingers must have traced…not even
once; never.

The last month of my life had seen me changing.
Restless nights, drowsy mornings, confused afternoons, lonely
evenings…I had experienced them all.

Nothing seemed to work—no amount of persuasion, no
amount of counselling by Boza and not even the regular phone
calls home. Every night I used to write her an e-mail, send her
a message on Facebook and wait for her to come online on
MSN, but to no avail.

'Aaryan,' someone called my name and knocked feverishly

on my door. I got up from my bed and quickly opened it.

'What the...

Boza barged into my room and closed the door quickly.

'Phew, that was dangerous. The campus police is around...' she paused to gather her breath and said, 'and why didn't you come for breakfast and why is there no light in this room? And why are you sitting all alone on a Sunday and...actually nothing.' She said, planting herself on my bed.

I latched the door; a girl seen in my room was the last thing I wanted after the last month's rendezvous with the headmaster.

'Oh my God...You are getting all the wrong signals here buddy—a girl and a boy, a dark, locked room, a lazy Sunday... no...' her attempt to induce some laughter was successful.

I switched on the light to show her what she was missing...

'Do you mind wearing something over those hideous red boxers,' she pretended to hide her face with a pillow.

'Why Boza baby, don't you like this?' I started to walk towards my bed.

'Oi....' she got up impulsively.

'Not oi...say ohh...aaah...,' I said and took the six steps that distanced us.

'Oh God..., Ew! You lord of lust,' she threw the pillow at me.

I caught it and moved forward to get hold of her legs... 'Oh yes, Boza...c'mon,' I said playfully.

'Stop it, JERK!' Boza tried to free herself and in the attempt, pinched me hard.

'Ohhh...I liked that,' I said and she gave me a solid push as I took her along in the fall.

The result—two best friends, a single bed...and then we started laughing hysterically—my hand now holding her waist, her hand pressed under my body weight, her left leg, under my right one, her right leg kicking me playfully, my left one, hanging from the bed.

'God, you haven't even brushed your teeth,' I said to Boza and our laughter increased only to slowly, slowly decrease into smiles and heavy sighs and then my face inched forward enough to rub my nose against hers. I saw her close her eyes; her hot breath engulfed my face, her lips dangerously close to mine.

'Hey...Aaryan! Open up,' Karan's unmistakable voice stopped me from kissing my best friend.

✿

'What took you so long...and yeah, Boza was searching for you all around,' Karan said, as soon as I opened the door.

'Thanks a ton, Karan. You're faster than an email,' said Boza, who had shifted from my bed to my study chair.

'Holy shit, Boza!' Karan gasped and repeated my action of latching the door quickly. 'Didn't our house parent see you?' he asked next.

Boza laughed artificially, unable to meet my eye. 'No he didn't...so Karan, where do you hide your smuggled cigarettes?'

'That's a secret, lady,' Karan replied in a Casanova's tone and Boza faked a smile.

'Okay, I'll catch you guys later,' she started to walk towards the door, without looking at me.

'So Aaryan, did you like your little surprise?' Karan suddenly asked and she stopped in the next breath.

'What surprise?' I asked timidly.

'Boza, didn't you give him the pamphlet?' Karan looked at Boza, then at me, trying to understand what was wrong here.

'Oh...yes, the pamphlet. This is for you, Aaryan,' she fished out something from her pocket, kept it on the nearest bed and left.

'What's up with you both?' Karan casually questioned as he took off his T-shirt, ready to go for a bath.

'Nothing...nothing at all,' I said, contemplating if I was lying or not!

The Pamphlet

Student Exchange Progamme
The United People's Organization invites students for a week-long student exchange programme to:

Malaysia
Thailand
Singapore
Duration: 31 March to 6 April 2010

Q.) WHO CAN APPLY?
Anyone who identifies with our ideals and ethos. So if you are in the age group of 16–18 years, are pursuing the International Baccalaureate Diploma Programme and fulfil our criteria, you have every reason to apply. To read more on our organization, please visit www.upo.org.

Q.) WHAT ARE WE LOOKING FOR?
1. Academically strong (with a grade A in the recent-most exams).
2. Politically aware (well versed with country history as you represent your country).
3. Socially concerned (participation in social endeavours and NGOs).
4. Physically active (sporting abilities).

Young student leaders will benefit from the enriched learning experience and will make use of the week of shared cultures, knowledge and much more.

Q.) HOW DO YOU APPLY?
Applications can be downloaded from the above mentioned website or a request can be made from the concerned school authorities.

Q.) WHAT IS THE SELECTION PROCESS?
1. Submission of application.
2. Written examination of short-listed candidates (English and G.K.).
3. Personal interviews.
Yes, you are on the flight!

Dates to Remember

15 October 2009: submission of forms.
10 November 2009: selected candidates are notified.
1 December 2009: written examination in Delhi & Mumbai.
15 December 2009: examination results declared; short-listed students notified.
1 January 2010: interviews with panel in Delhi & Mumbai.
1 February 2010: names of selected students declared.

Aaryan
THE PRESENT

'You wanted to know why I came here. Here, this is your answer' I reached for the little shoulder bag I was carrying and took out a certificate.

Tanie read it and gasped, 'The student exchange programme.

I smiled faintly, 'Yes, the same programme.'

'So, you did manage to get selected, but how?' she ended

in a surprised tone.

I gave her a raised-eyebrow look.

'I mean, weren't you the not-so-academic and the social-service type?' she said in her defence.

I laughed heartily.

'What?' she demanded.

'You just sounded like Boza...' I said.

She suddenly jumped on her seat and clapped her hands, 'Yeah, yeah, yeah! I almost forgot. What about Boza? You both were about to kiss and then Ishita! Did you meet her now that you are in Singapore?'

I laughed again, 'Well, you seem too interested in my world,' I said and crumpled the disposable coffee cup.

'Spare the suspense, Aaryan! Tell me. They haven't even announced anything about our flight,' she said.

I looked at my watch, 'Okay, but on one condition only,' I said slowly.

'What is it?'

'For my story comes your story,' I said softly again.

She kept silent for some seconds, debating internally. 'What makes you think I have a story to share?' she asked.

'Hmmmm...destiny.'

'Destiny?' she asked with surprise.

'Yes...destiny.' Couldn't she see the connect—the same book, an MUN and the note.

She sat there silently, wondering if she had made a mistake by sitting with me in the first place.

'You don't have to look so troubled,' I said, trying to make her understand.

'Oh...No no, not at all, yaar...,' she said, embarrassed.

'Yes...so, how did I bag the student exchange?' I said and again let myself immerse in the sea of my memories.

Aaryan
THE PAST

'Karan!' I shouted and banged the toilet door, after I had read, re-read and again read the pamphlet.

He did not reply.

'Karan! Open up, or I'll break the door,' I said aloud in excitement. This was my chance; yes, this was it.

'Aaryan, I was in the middle of my bubble bath,' a water-drenched, soap-smeared, towel-wrapped Karan lamented, after opening the door.

'Dude! Did you read this? This is like so fucking awesome! I am going to Singapore now. Ishita…here I come,' I shouted at the top of my voice and hugged him tightly.

'Uh…yes, I know,' Karan said, trying to push me away.

We both laughed and I dashed to my laptop to open the website and check out the details of the programme.

🐜

'Finally, I found you. When did you leave the room?' a dried and dressed Karan asked me. I was sitting in the school cafeteria, having lunch with Batra and Andrew, our classmate.

Andrew finished his lunch and excused himself while Karan came and occupied the same seat.

'Oi Aaryan, did you check the site?' he asked.

'Is there a new porn website?' Batra excitedly interjected.

'No man…it's the student exchange programme website,' I groaned.

'The what?' Batra asked confused.

'Actually Aaryan, everyone was supposed to get them in the assembly…Boza sneaked out a pamphlet from the Activity Coordinator's room when she went to her today morning,'

Karan explained.

Boza—time and again, she had to prove that I was lucky to have her in my life. In all the excitement that had followed, I had completely forgotten of the awkward moment between us some time back. I hadn't seen her ever since.

'Where is Boza?'

'I saw her in the soccer field.' Karan informed me.

'Thank you. Karan, come along then,' I got up and tagged a reluctant Karan to the field.

༄

We found her on the soccer field. It really isn't hard to spot the only girl among twenty odd boys.

'I never knew, Boza could kick some ball,' it was Karan's turn to act surprised. We were standing near one end of the field.

A volcano of fury inside me erupted suddenly. 'Boza Korbi!' I spewed lava with all my might. The game stopped, everybody looking at us from a distance.

'Are you alright?' Karan carefully asked me.

'Boza, come here!' I shouted again and after two seconds, I saw a figure run across the field to where we stood.

'Why are you shouting my name, Aaryan?' she asked us.

'Since when did you start playing soccer?' I demanded angrily.

'There is no need to shout,' she said calmly.

'Twenty guys and you alone...what are you trying to prove?' I couldn't control the pitch.

I saw Boza turn around and walk away from me.

'Where do you think you are going?' I started walking behind her. She didn't reply.

'Boza...you have to answer me,' I said, holding her arm from behind. She jerked my hand, trying to set herself free.

'Everything alright here?' Chloe ma'am, who was returning towards the faculty quarters, asked.

'Y…yes…ma'am. Just a minor friendship fight,' Karan, who had silently been following us, came to our rescue.

She looked at Boza and then me and addressed her question to Boza, 'Are you sure? You don't look good to me.'

Boza cleared her throat to speak, 'Ma'am, everything is fine…it's just two hours of soccer in the sun,' she said and managed a fake smile.

Chloe still unsure, interrogated us for a few minutes and finally left.

'Boza, listen, can we please talk amicably?' The few minutes of interrogation had helped me cool my mind.

'Was I the one who was shouting in the first place, Karan?' she asked Karan.

'I…no,' the mediator always gets screwed.

'Fine…I know I was shouting, Karan, but you tell me, what point can a girl prove by playing alone among so many boys and that also in such a skimpy attire?' I asked him of her.

'Karan…do you think this is skimpy?' she asked. 'But Karan…'

'Shut up…you two,' he said and marched off.

'C'mon Boza, you were about to kiss me in my room some time back and now you go out playing with guys…You are nothing short of a…sss,' I stopped. Thaasshhhhh—a sound slap restricted the word.

'I can't believe you just said that…Aaryan, after all these years…I…,' her voice broke. 'You know what? Boys like you can never fall in love…you lust Ishita…nothing else and I am glad that she hasn't replied to your e-mail till today because this is what you are worth…Aaryan Gill,' she spat to show me my worth. 'If you don't believe me, go try your luck with the student exchange programme. Go to Singapore and face it... you are a jerk, a lame mother-fucking jerk.'

Thaaasshh...another slap was meted out that day. A guy had slapped a girl.

'One thing, I promise you Boza, I will get through the fucking student exchange programme and get it in writing from Ishita that she loves me, because I love her...something you definitely won't understand.'

And I walked off from there in a huff.

Tanie
THE PRESENT

'Here,' Aaryan handed me a tissue. Eyes are like prostitutes—they reveal more than they can conceal. I took the tissue and used it to the fullest. He smiled and closed his eyes for a minute.

'It's hard to run away from them,' he said, after he found me staring at him.

'Tears and memories,' I replied. He gave the faintest of smiles.

'So Tanie, you still don't have anything to share?' his tone seemed to pierce me through. Sumer's note was in my pocket. It screamed for a reply and it rightly deserved one.

An announcement cut me from sharing my tale: 'All passengers travelling to New Delhi via Air India are requested to move to Terminal 3. We apologize once again for the delay.'

'Destiny,' I heard Aaryan say in a mocking tone as we got up and picked up our bags to leave.

🐾

'C-45,' I said to the pretty airhostess.

'This way,' she guided me and I started following her, each

step distancing me from where Aaryan was seated. 'C-114,' he had announced and sat down some five minutes ago. The seat next to him was occupied already.

'Ma'am, your seat,' the airhostess said and I looked down the alley once. Unable to spot him in the almost full-to-capacity plane, I sat down on my seat, feeling uneasy, unheard.

I saw the airhostess help someone with his luggage; her round butt and short skirt would have made Sumer drool. I smiled till a hopeless feeling of despair overtook me again.

I fastened my seat belt and forcefully shut my eyes to snap all my connections with this world. Even in the cold darkness, Sumer's memories didn't leave me. The first time we met... the Sunday tuition, Maths test, the infamous sneak out...the Friendship Day surprise...the innumerable times he helped me meet Rehaan, the boy who I thought I loved till that fateful day.

'Memories...they never leave you,' Aaryan's voice automatically opened my eyes.

'Hh...hi...,' I replied. He was seated next to me. 'How long have you been sitting here?' I asked him foolishly.

'Hmm...for a while,' he replied and smiled. 'Why didn't you tap me or something?' I asked.

'I enjoyed looking at your expressions,' he said and instantly added in a defensive protocol, 'not in that way!'

I laughed out aloud.

'Hmm...finally someone appreciates my sense of humour,' he joked.

'Not really. You reminded me of someone.'

'Oh...okay,' he shifted in his seat. 'So...,' he said as if he expected something.

'Nothing...I think I need some sleep,' I said and closed my eyes, knowing that sleep was the last thing that could happen to me now.

11

Barely Buddies

Tanie
THE PAST

May
The first time we meet, he picks me up in his arms!

So let us begin from the start.

Difficult it was not to not break into a grin when your supposed English tuition teacher comes up with one-liners which can easily put the makers of *Webster* and *Oxford* to shame. It's a talent only few possess and a fewer master.

In every Indian school-going teenager's life comes a year when they realize that *Titanic* could possibly be the last movie they have seen, when their parents buy them inspirational posters from the street vendors, when they develop muscles even without working out because they carry weights the whole day to different torture chambers, when they suspiciously find their cell phone ringing in their mothers purse or their father's cupboard every time they are unable to find it, when teachers indulge in homework homicide on only one pretext, when they can recite the titles of every guidebook available in the market, when their room posters are hidden by animated schedules and time-tables, when only their class is called to school every Saturday, when they have more exams than holidays, when teachers glare when they fight and argue that checking isn't fair, when Diwali becomes the last festival of the year, when New Year brings in no cheer, when birthday treats are delayed for days, when the summer vacations are meant to take crash or trash courses in subjects like English, when relationships begin and end at the hub of socializing (tuition), when they are warned and reminded that one March would change their march in life. It was this year in my life, the year which had that something extra attached to everything. It was the time when my Facebook had dedicated groups on how Boards suck.

The first day of summer vacation and suddenly there was a cynical cerebral imbalance in Mom's mind. 'Tanie, there's this lady just down the lane who is starting with a crash course in English today. Be ready at five.' She had literally dropped a bomb at lunch.

'But Mom, why English?' I had protested. 'Why not?' she had shot back.

'It's easy; I won't need extra help.'

'Consider it as guidance,' she had offered.

'Mom, you are so stubborn!' I had shouted as the last retort.

'I am your Mom after all, right?' In any case I loved her wit.

'Fine, but only for a month.'

So here I was in the Nazi enclosure with five other Jews waiting to be tortured by a Nazi, who evidently believed in joke-poison. Needless to say, her venomous jokes stung.

'Today we all will start with *Julius Caesar*,' the Nazi announced. 'I want you people to do role-play, so who will be the narrator—Caesar, his wife and the other characters?'

'I will be the narrator,' the liberally-oiled, two-plaited,

salwar-kameez-clad girl I had seen around in the sector excitedly volunteered. Phew, she was like so strained!

'What about the other roles?' the Nazi wanted to know. Everyone started to look away, '*Bachcha*, you all have a young voice, strong and powerful like Pappu dear from the song.' I forced a laugh on hearing similar sounds.

'Fine, I will leave it to you. Just read when your turn comes,' she suggested.

The gas inlets had opened because of a Jew traitor. The oil princess began in her squeaky voice as everyone turned their books to the designated page, 'All hail Caesar!'

'Good evening,' an unidentified loud sound buzzed at the garage-converted chamber-door. Everyone began to laugh.

Meanwile a new entrant made his presence felt.

'Come in. Welcome Caesar, you are late,' Jasmine (the Nazi) said with mixed annoyance and sweetness.

'I am sorry...I thought my Mom had told you that I was going to be a bit late...we just moved in actually.'

'Oh yes, I forgot. What did you say was your name?' Jasmine asked, trying to hide her fault.

'Err...I never said anything till now.'

Now everyone gave a genuine laugh. 'I am Sumer,' he added innocently, sensing that he had offended the teacher even before she had begun to teach.

'Go, sit and don't be late again,' she ordered and the next thing I knew, the new entrant was walking in my direction.

The first thing I noticed about him as he approached closer, was his height, the extra-long Tommy Hilfiger T-shirt ended just where the extra low-waist denims began to fall, giving way to worn-out branded slippers—pretty neat compared to the other duds who considered themselves dudes sitting in the room. He came right next to me and sat down.

❧

My cell phone vibrated a minute after I stepped back into civilization, outside the Nazi camp. It was Rehaan. 'Finally, free?' he asked.

'Yup, just starting to walk back home. I needed some fresh air; this tuition is deadly, yaar,' I answered.

'Aww...want to go for a drive. I can pick you from our meeting place.' He meant the ground near my house.

'Yeah! So, when Mom comes to know her all-girls convent-going daughter is going out with a guy celebrating his eighteenth birthday in a few months, she can get reason enough to take away my cell phone, sabotage my outings and drive me everywhere around,' I said.

'So tell her,' he joked.

'Surely, your eternal wish of not getting any calls from me during the night or I not keeping tab on your whereabouts will definitely get fulfilled,' I lamented.

'So when do I get to see you?'

'This weekend or...(thud!). Hey, I dropped my books. Will call you when I reach home,' I said and disconnected the call.

As I bent down to gather the scattered BBC assignments, some guy from the tuition whose name I never bothered to find out, zoomed by a millimetre's distance on his black Honda Activa.

His mission was complete; I was now sitting on the road on all my fours. 'Asshole,' I shouted back in reaction.

'Here, let me help you,' a friendly voice said from behind, the air suddenly turning scented. 'It's just not my day,' I grumbled inaudibly as I allowed my petite body to be picked up by the tower in one swift try.

'Phew, that was easier than I thought,' he said jokingly. He picked up the books to hand them over to me.

'Hi, I mean thanks, I am Tanie,' I managed to mumble extending my hand.

'I'm Sumer,' he replied, embracing it.

'Yes, I know,' I replied rather quickly.

'Okay,' he seemed bewildered.

'So you just moved in here?' I asked.

'Yeah, from Gurgaon. I moved into house number 143,' he informed.

'Okay,' I smiled and continued walking towards my home, house no. 142.

⅜

'How was tuition?' Mom's voice stopped me as I opened door of my room. I was in a hurry as Rehaan didn't like to wait for long.

'I am alive,' I answered quickly, looking at my dust covered hands.

'Aarti aunty has finished setting up her home,' Mom said, taking me away from my personal paradise.

'I know, her son has shifted in too,' I informed her.

'You do?' Mom stopped me again from closing the door. I was getting impatient now.

'Yes, I met her son at the tuition at your recommendation, I suppose,' I added sarcastically.

'And?' Mom questioned again.

'And he virtually picked me up in his arms, Mom,' I shouted, getting irritated. He had in a way though!

'She has invited us for dinner,' Mom said, still maintaining her cool.

'Enjoy yourself,' I snapped and shut the door to her dying voice which sounded something like 'I said "us".'

Aarti aunty was Mom's new-found friend. Since the last two weeks, they had practically spent every evening setting up her home. It had all started with the customary cup of coffee, the slight alteration being that she had come to offer instead of taking. 'It's straight from Brazil,' she had announced merrily, informing us in a way that her husband as a Navy captain travelled a lot. During her short talk on the first day, which seemed to go on approximately till seven in the evening, she had mentioned about her son living with her in-laws in Gurgaon till the whole shifting was to be done.

She had repeatedly praised Mom on her taste in almost everything (even though she hadn't had anything to eat, diet-conscious, you see). She had evidently won over Mom, so when Mom volunteered to help her and her lost husband, who had relocated to Chandigarh because he wanted to invest in property in Punjab, I wasn't surprised. Why would I be? It obviously meant more time to freely talk with Rehaan.

Rehaan—I quickly searched for his contact name 'Ruchika' (I never took chances since mom knew all my 'limited' male friends by their names) and dialled it.

'What took you so long?'

I had expected this.

'Sorry, got late in coming back.' And then I narrated the whole incident about falling on the road, about the local jerk and finally Mom and the dinner (I hadn't mentioned anything about Sumer till then).

'So this guy needs to be taught how to drive?' Rehaan said in his characteristic bossy tone—the tone I just drooled on.

'No, don't *jaan*, it's okay. If he troubles again, I will let you know, *pucca*,' I promised him.

'And when will you come back from this stupid dinner of yours?' he asked with some irritation.

'Who says I am going?' I asked.

'Great! So we get time to talk then or should I come?' he said hopefully.

'No, don't come, its just next door and maybe, I think I should go. I met my new neighbour today; their son I mean. He is in Class X too—tall, handsome and kind of...' I left the sentence hanging midway.

'Kind of...?' Rehaan asked impatiently. Jealousy is a human trait after all.

'Kind of nice,' I wanted to say 'hot', but knowing of his historic mood swings I chose not to.

'He better be just that,' he said possessively. I loved it when he ascertained his right over me.

'And did I tell you he picked me up in his arms today?' I said and started laughing. 'Hello? Hello? Rehaan?' he had disconnected the call. I dialled his number again.

'I was joking *jaan*. Why do you always do this to me?' I lied to him. I didn't want to, but I just did.

'Okay, sorry baby. I just can't (beep) stand you talking about (beep) some other guy,' he said exactly what I wanted to hear. 'Who is calling?' he wanted to know the reasons of the beeps, the call waiting.

'Wait, let me see,' I said and checked it. 'Oh my gosh! It's Mom,' I shrieked, thinking of the next punishment for banging (or closing) the door that was going to be announced soon. 'I'll call you in some time,' I cut the call, before he could say 'bye and I picked up Mom's call.

'Yes, Mom?' I said in a bored-to-death tone.

'Who were you talking to?' Mom asked politely. 'Your son-in-law,' I said in the same tone.

'Oh really, how nice!' she said sarcastically. No value for truth, huh!

'So, I was thinking you should wear your black dress tonight,' Mom said in her never-to-stop trying manner.

'To bed?' I wasn't that naive either.

She took a deep breath, 'No Tanie, for the dinner. Come for your Dad's sake at least,' she said politely.

'Even Dad won't go,' I told her.

'He will,' she said in fixed tone.

'He won't,' I said more forcefully, being well aware of his not-interested approach to socializing. 'Let's bet,' I threw in the ace now.

'Fine. Come down then. He should be back soon.' Mom agreed, she didn't have any choice anyway.

'Okay,' I said and ended the call, debating on whether to call Rehaan once I knew tonight's fate or just call him now and let Mom and Dad decide my fate. I chose on the first option and got up to go downstairs.

'It is simply healthy social interaction,' Mom had again begun her campaign over tea, as we sat waiting for Dad.

'Yes, gossiping about how maids and husbands and how children torture you poor overburdened souls and, how can I forget, Boards and studies and how today's generation chooses buddies,' I said taking a sip from my iced tea.

'Was that intentionally rhymed? I knew English tuition would help,' only mothers can make a heated argument seem like a cool, deliberated discussion.

'Ding-dong', we heard the bell together. 'I am home,' Dad began with his customary announcement. To my surprise, Mom did not get up, nor did I hear the part of routine shout, 'Rani, *sahib ke liye paani lao.*' Fuck, something wasn't right here.

'Hi, love,' he called out merrily to Mom. She didn't respond. Wait a minute, he was carrying a bouquet of carnations (Mom's favourite). So they had fought again. He reached the living room.

Mom pretended to take no notice of the flowers and like some old, crappy, romantic saga, Dad placed them in front of her. Mom picked them up and smiled.

'How mushy,' I mumbled, suddenly remembering how Rehaan had done the same for me the last time we had fought. A passionate lip-lock had followed. 'Excuse me, but we have a master bedroom here,' I said loud enough, lest history would repeat itself.

Mom blushed. 'Tanie, did someone tell you I own this house?' my helplessly romantic Dad had a lifelong-fractured, funny bone.

'You surely do,' I said and got up from my chair to hug him.

'Let's go out for dinner,' Dad suggested.

'We are invited for dinner at Aarti's place,' Mom said, looking at me.

'Who is Aarti?' Dad asked, bewildered.

'Suraj, see you don't even know about my friends... Well they are our new neighbours,' Mom replied in an accusing tone. So this was the moment—Go for it Dad!

'Fine, I'll order a wine bottle,' he smiled to Mom. She smiled back and then turned to me, 'So Tanie, why don't you wear your black dress tonight?'

Why don't I wear black thongs, Mom? 'Sure,' I forced a smile.

'Traitor,' I accused Dad, after Mom left to get ready five minutes later.

'All is fair in love and war, Tanie and I have already had one with your Mom today morning.'

G...r...e...a...t, my Dad had decided to play a good husband now.

'Fine, but I'll come back right after dinner, even if you want to stay on,' I said and walked to my room, thinking of what to wear as even Sumer would be there.

※

'Ding-dong!'

'Mom, bell *bhi* same *hai*,' I quickly whispered in her ear, fearing the door would open. It didn't take long for my fears to turn into reality.

'Hi, everyone!' Aarti aunty seemed to explode with enthusiasm. 'Tanie, you've come too. How nice! Sumer was telling me about you. Hi, there, Mr Brar!'

Even Dad wasn't spared as we were swept in by the wave of excitement. One look at the house and anybody who knew her would say: Mom was here—the same characteristic interplay of light shades, the ultra-modern interiors, the extra details to mastered futility like scented candles and curios. It was like a home few steps away from home.

'Hello there, young lady,' Sumer's Dad startled me.

'Oh, hullo uncle,' I literally had to crane my neck in respect. So this is where he got that extra-long factor.

'Why don't you go up and ask Sumer to come down? Second room from the left,' he added, before I could say anything. Dad shot me an apologetic look from behind and turned back to head to the drawing room with the rest of the oldies.

It takes enormous effort to climb up the stairs in high pointed heels; it took more than that to digest what came next.

'Not bad at all,' I observed as I stared at a beautiful girl wearing chic semi-formal pants and a black shirt and sporting a carefully done careless bun. Guess what? She was me. The king-sized mirror kept outside his room shone more than it should have. '*Bang-bang.*' Suddenly loud music began to blare through the almost empty floor, breaking the poised and subtle miss evening moment.

'Umm...hello,' I knocked on the DJ's door. No reply. '*Bang,*

bang yeah!' 'Sumer?' I knocked a little harder. No reply. Bang, bang, boom! 'Anybody there?'

My potentially aggravated frustration ended with a kinetic bang on the door this time. The song stopped. 'Oops,' I muttered realizing why time as given in physics had to prove itself. '*Cut my life into pieces, this is my last retort...*'—a new song began.

'That's it. I am barging inside,' I spoke loudly, hoping he could hear. '*Suffocation ahh, suffocation ohh, suffocation yeah...*' the song that was playing should have been an embarrassment aah, embarrassment ohh, embarrassment yeah...

A tall, brown-coloured ape was dancing in front of me. He looked like a wild, prehistoric man but they didn't wear red Tommy boxers, nor did they have a tattoo right under the navel which extended into...stop! His naked, miserly-sculpted chest and long legs were too much of an exposure for my naked eyes. He suddenly turned around, his curly locks bouncing in coordination. 'Oh hi, Tanie,' he shouted, trying to outdo the music.

I was too dumbstruck to react and this guy thought it was perfectly normal to dance wearing nothing but your briefs in front of guests, or girls, or me. 'Tanie!' he shrieked.

'Huh, welcome back, modern ape.' He quickly ran to the toilet, kicking his pod speakers on the way.

There are Kodak moments—moments which cannot be framed and then there are moments which we both had experienced.

'*Beta*, where's Sumer?' Aarti aunty asked as I returned back to the drawing room, alone. Wine and Jagjit Singh's voice had overpowered their loud monotones. I wanted to say, 'Probably hanging from his exhaust fan', but settled for 'getting ready'.

'Oh, sit with us then.' It was Mom this time. Her eyes spoke of her curiosity; she longed to see Aarti's son. Dad and uncle were talking animatedly about some stock market cycle, when he came down.

'There he is,' announced Aarti aunty with wine's shortlived effect wearing out.

'Young man, it is indecent to keep a young, beautiful lady waiting,' Sumer's Dad spoke in a manner patented by officers alone.

'Sorry, Dad, I was changing,' he said, glancing at me through the corner of his eye. The mandatory salutations followed.

Surprise! Surprise! Mom seemed to be pleased with the courteous, feet-touching boy. 'No, no, *beta!*' she tried to stop him.

'No, Smiley, he should learn,' Aarti aunty beamed. He had evidently been bred well, after all.

'What will you have, aunty?' he asked my mother like a practising butler.

'Oh nothing, *beta*,' Mom gave me the see-and-learn look.

What—I gave her the look in reply.

'Hi, Tanie,' he came up to me now and extended his hand. Mother Earth open your heart and imbibe me in your soul!

'Hi, Sumer,' I said after an awkward pause.

'So, can I get you something? Coke or lime or a breezer?'

Ha, so he wasn't all that saintly! I quickly glanced towards Mom, who seemed in a sort of shock, while Aarti aunty showed no change in her expression.

They were cool parents. Look and learn, Mom, I thought. 'Tanie *beta*, what will you have?' Dad asked me. I bet he wanted to know if I would choose an alcoholic beverage or something lame and light.

'I'll have a coke, Sumer,' I said, faking an Oscar-winning smile.

'I'll guide you to the bar,' he said.

'Yes, Tanie, go along.' Miracle! Did Mom just tell me to

go have a drink (okay, its just coke) with a guy? I had to laugh this out.

'Sure,' I said, getting the perfect opportunity.

❦

'So the tattoo; is that for real?' I asked, breaking the ice physically and literally, while he poured coke in one glass and took out a breezer from the ice bucket. I so envied him.

'Oh that?' he said, after taking a sip from the bottle. He came closer to whisper now, 'Actually only Liaka knows about it till now,' he said and grinned sheepishly. 'She is my girl, two years and five months,' he added proudly.

'*Wait till you come to know that I have a Labrador whose name is also Liaka.*' I surpressed the chuckle accompanying my thought. 'Aww, that's sweet, but why there? I mean the position,' I asked next.

'Oh, she loves to see it there,' he said, not realizing what it implied on further dwelling. 'I mean,' he became all red. So he did realize. 'I mean, she suggested me to get it done there.'

I just smiled, taking another sip. 'So, won't she be jealous now?' I teasingly asked.

'Of?' he looked confused.

'The fact that another girl just saw it.'

'She will understand, yaar,' he replied coolly.

'Understand what?' I pressed again.

'That we are barely buddies,' he replied.

I laughed, he laughed, problem solved.

Tanie
THE PRESENT

Finally, I opened my eyes. A minute, an hour or sometime in

between, I had no clue after how long! I had walked down the memory lane in the familiar darkness and forgotten the path back.

The seat next to me was vacant again. Aaryan had gone back.

When? I didn't know.

Why? I didn't want to know.

He must have sat for a while, waiting patiently for me to open my eyes, my mouth and Sumer's note.

I should just walk up to him...shouldn't I? I questioned myself silently. And then say what? Hello, Mr Aaryan! Unlike you, I kissed my best friend and then broke up with my boyfriend... No, I should push the note in his hand and find a way to jump off the plane...he'll be able to find Sumer and tell him my dilemma or perhaps I should just flush down the note and let Aaryan, Sumer, Rehaan, everyone go to hell. But then, I'll meet them there again, after death. Sheesh...

'What the hell?' I gasped loud enough to invite surprise, concern and even mocking stares from the people seated around me. Even the airhostess walking by gave the brief, plastic-plastered smile.

I covered my face with my hands in embarrassment, thinking it all was just a bad dream.

'Ramdev again?' I heard Aaryan's friendly voice.

I looked up instantly and questioned in a sheepish tone 'Err...was I that loud?'

'Yes!' he said and added, 'just kidding' after two seconds.

'I was just walking by,' he ended.

'Going somewhere?' I asked foolishly. Every path in a plane leads to the toilet. Period.

'Yeah...to the pilot's cabin. Thought I'd drop by and say hi or something,' he said wittily.

'Very funny...hey, what do you have in your hand over

there?' My gaze fell upon a worn-out book which his left hand seemed to hold possessively.

'Oh this?' He looked pensive for a moment and then smiled fishily, 'It's just a book,' he said and winked, his positive behaviour diffusing in the cold air of awkwardness that I had stupidly created around myself.

'You could sit here if you want to...after you are done with the toilet, I mean,' I said sheepishly. He smiled and moved on to the toilet, only to return and sit after two minutes.

Five painful minutes passed in silence, the new language of our communication. He turned away from me and opened the mysterious book to read it.

'Uh...Ummm...Aaryan, did you not try to talk to each other again?' I asked carefully, some two minutes later.

He closed the book and kept it securely away from me, between the arm-rest and his lap. 'Who?' he shot me a confused look.

'Boza and You,' I said urgently.

Every question put to him satiated the hungry answers of my life.

He opened his mouth to speak and then kept quiet. He repeated it again and then suddenly closed his eyes. I got scared. 'Aaryan...are you alright?' I reached for his shoulder.

'I am a murderer...I murdered our friendship,' he said slowly and breathed deeply. I reached for the water bottle and opened it for him.

'Fine now?' I asked, after he had emptied half of it.

'I am a murderer...I murdered our friendship,' he repeated again.

'Why do you say that?' I gasped. The ghosts of his past were haunting my present. His story, so like mine and dangerously close to reality, was being revealed to someone I was going to be.

'Boza…on Dad's birthday, she got a wine bottle delivered at home with my name. She knew that Dad and I didn't exactly share an ideal bond but still she didn't want to give up any chance. She truly cared for me and I was always a jerk. She even doctored my attendance record, when I was applying for the student exchange programme. She even gave me apology cards—she didn't want to lose me and I didn't even wish her on her birthday.'

Sumer had decided to play peacemaker and had sent Mom her favourite flowers by my name after Mom and I had had an epic war.

'How did you come to know all this?' I asked him next.

'Chimmy told me and I could recognize her handwriting easily. You know what? Dad and I talked for an hour on his birthday…like man to man. It felt nice,' he smiled.

Mom had come into my room and hugged me. She had shown me the carnations and kissed me on my cheek. Sumer's not so evolved handwriting had been a give away. Courtesy him, Mom and I had talked about everything—from boys to new bras that day, woman to woman. It had felt nice.

'So that's about it…' he clapped his hands lightly. 'I started studying like an ass, joined three social groups on campus and even went to this orphanage for social service. I started reading Indian history and current affairs became completely isolated from my friends and lost my best friend and a part of me… but then, my dream began to take shape. Ishita had finally started replying to my e-mails. I got selected for the interview round and somehow managed to charm the selection panel. When they asked me which country I would like to go to, I said "Singapore" in the next second.'

He ended his story and looked at me hopefully.

'Well, I also have a story to share, but there's a condition.'

'What?' he smiled and asked.

'You will have to answer a question in the end.'

'That seems simple,' he replied.

'Not exactly,' I shot back.

'Hmmm...maybe! But then we always have destiny...the biggest answer to all questions, or the biggest question to all answers.'

I tried hard to absorb and make sense of whatever he meant but like always, I flashed a pretentious smile and began with my tale.

12

Barely Buddies to Besharam Best Friends

Tanie
THE PAST

November
When we became besharam best friends.

Imprinted in history, guided by practice, arrives a morning after six fervent days, soaked in academic pressure and nights leaking in graphic pleasure.

Early morning, while the world student population is lulled by the conspiring contentment of idling away the next twenty-four hours, young Indian blood pulsates to rise.

Armed with sleek and sophisticated ammunition, ranging from a Reynolds racer to an Ad gel achiever, sharp geometric weapons and life-changing blank sheets, they gather at algebraic army camps to learn it the hard way.

You cannot fail, yet passing is a high-altitude dream. Time and again your endurance is put to test by a diabolically designed question paper. You are subjected to inhuman 'problem sums'.

But you have to be prepared to survive the vicious cycle of pained idolism. Don't be disheartened even if you weekly sacrifice your state of suspended sensory and motor activity for such futility. Remember, you are blessed with a perfect platform where to proclaim patriotism also means glamourizing the zero, once invented by an ancient son of our motherland.

'Good morning,' I kissed my mobile.

'Wow, this is some kinky alarm!' Sumer commented.

'Shut up. Not you; it's Sumer baby,' I replied.

'Oh, okay. What's the time?' Rehaan's groggy yet sexy voice worked like coffee fumes for my drowsy eyes.

'Its 9 a.m., baby, I'm heading back home,' I sang. 'What? One second, hang on,' I put Rehaan on hold. 'Sumer, can you turn the volume down!' I shouted at my new-found driver, who shot back an evil look. *'Resume'.*

'Yeah! Sorry! Fine, go and take a shower...no, I won't join you,' I alternated between blushes and giggles.

'Ahem,' Sumer began, 'as indulgent you are in your Sunday morning telephonic treasures, I suggest you use some protection too,' he warned in a news reporter's voice.

'What?' I exclaimed loud enough for both the important guys in my life to hear.

'Strap your seatbelt, Tanie. I am an underage driver,' he grimaced at my low intelligence level.

'Rehaan's asking you to chill. He's seventeen and drives too,' I passed the message like a proud parrot.

Suddenly a chill began to creep inside the November warm and cozy black Honda Civic. Great, he had pulled down all the windows now!

'What?' I multitasked, answering Rehaan and signalling Sumer.

'Trying to chill,' Sumer replied and I burst out laughing.

'Baby, no, nothing is funny. I'll call you once I'm home, 'bye!' I disconnected the phone before our customary hour of saying goodbyes in a hundred possible ways could be initiated. 'Sumer, you are so...,' I turned to shout at him.

'Chilled out,' he completed the phrase, grinning back. 'Now let me verse you with real mush.' He switched on the CD player and in no time a sweet romantic track started to play.

A cool Sunday morning garnished with perfect music and served in a comfortable drive forced me to dip my feet in nostalgic waters. With my smile striated by falling hair and head turned away from Sumer towards the world which we never cared about, memories of the last four months of (im) moral but honest, (im) perfect but cherished moments with my new driver and best friend flashed before my eyes.

Even Einstein would be baffled at the growth of potential momentum, the lone case of induction of friction and increase in the intensity of velocity between us. Four months ago we barely knew each other even though he had practically bared his heart, soul and a little more to me on our first meeting.

A month of walking back together from the tuition (till mid June), the weekend dinners (till now) had resulted in my mother having a strong affinity towards him.

As the leaves of time flew, the polite smiles metamorphosed into genuine acknowledgements, reaching the pinnacles of shouts from one rooftop to the other. His overtly witty attitude contrasting with his down-to-earth nature was one of the main reasons for us to gel. He was an adorable pest, a fabled perfectionist who posed great competition to sugar for its characteristics of deadly sweetness and mixing quickly and easily in unknown waters. It took him little time to befriend 'the people at his new school'; it took him even lesser to be counted among cute guys in the gossip circles of my school.

His guy friends and my girlfriends were involved in, as parents would term, 'unhealthy friendships' which gave reason enough for us to catch movies together or enter and walk out of birthdays pool in for gifts. This star basketball player had danced into my life with an ease which often propelled us to believe that this perhaps was destined to be.

Now Sumer was part of my world. He did everything from completing my English homework to fetching Rehaan when his car broke down; to helping us meet, to pressing the string of friendship with him. He had slowly, and surely, cemented a relationship which a simple word like 'friendship' couldn't contain.

Still, we weren't angels, for angels never indulged in lewd cross-talk about biological cycles and nor did they discuss the latest X-rated sites on the internet.

My eyelids shut to the world that was and opened to the world I sat thinking about. Flash, the scene came across as a recollection of joy and agony in its deepest form.

The first time I asked him to walk Liaka, my bitch, was some time in June.

'I hate dogs,' he said, his forehand glistening with a sudden brightness of pearls.

'But Liaka is a bitch.'

'And you're bitchy,' he had tried his best to snap back, understanding the dig.

'I think they are lovely,' I had continued, playing with her leash.

'Only till they bite,' his expression spoke of an unpleasant experience.

'At least my Liaka doesn't bite...she's a good bitch, you see.'

The pained look on his face had suddenly turned the atmosphere in a light shade of grey. It was brightened by Liaka's bark as if in agreement with her praise after a few moments.

'See, even Liaka likes me; I am just so irresistible.' He was too sweet to let anger enter his emotional sphere for long.

I stroked Liaka repeatedly, waiting to see how long it would take the petrified soul to pee. 'You like it the doggy way?' I questioned him, expunging the last iota of grim pleasure from the situation.

'Yeah, Liaka loves it...I didn't expect you to be so naive, Tanie.'

Fine, so he had a thing with words.

'You're sick, Sumer,' I had replied to his obvious mention which strongly suggested of his glorified animal instincts.

'Birds of a feather flock together,' his coolness had pawned me.

'Wait, I'll turn her in, but Liaka will be jealous if we go for the walk by ourselves,' I joked, trying my best to match his antics.

🐾

As the road moved along, all mortar material passed and the momentary sunlight entering my eye gave way to a dark comfort again.

So, you were sneaking out?' Sumer's melodramatic monotone buzzed in my ears.

It was probably the last Sunday of July. The sky was faintly traced with a little twinkle and the moon was playing hide and seek with the clouds, probably ashamed at the intent of my meeting Rehaan at 3 a.m. or the extent to which our 'little interaction' could end.

The small screen of my cell provided the only light to the otherwise metaphoric and literal darkness, as I stood on my roof, without any guilt, logic or fear of getting caught scaling down, probably 25 feet or less.

The rope was ready. Five bed sheets were fastened and tied

in knots as strong as the ones I was feeling in my stomach. Still everything was almost perfect. With no faunal trace around and silence silencing everything except my heart: excited beat, nervous burst, the involuntary response being the only hurdle to my voluntary decision and continued action.

Now all I had to do was to wait till my phone would buzz and announce the bliss that would follow.

B...u...z...z! I answered without bothering to read the name being flashed. 'Hey, I am on my roof; just need to climb down straight in your heart,' I whispered seductively.

'That I can see darling, turn left,' a familiar voice unfamiliar to the situation answered.

'Oh fuck! Sumer,' I gasped, fumbling with my cell.

'Expecting someone else, are we?' he questioned.

'You're awake...why?' was all that I could manage in acute desperation.

'Yes, up, awake and straight...I asked you to turn left.'

I followed his instructions as a strong flash from his cell enlightened me of his position.

'But it's so dark. How could you see me?' I questioned with curiosity and genuine interest, lest history would repeat itself some other day.

'Initially, I just saw a white-coloured snake flying,' he replied.

'Oh that is my rope,' I cut him, regretting instantly why I couldn't shut up when required.

He just laughed 'What?'

'Nothing, I am just...okay Rehaan is coming to pick me up,' I blurted out.

'Tanie! There are better ways to commit suicide... But don't, I still need you? We have to paint my room, remember,' he joked in his characteristic style.

'Don't worry. Mom-Dad won't know, and I'll be back

before five,' I replied, incorrectly interpreting his comical yet practical statement.

'Oh, I hope you didn't lace the drinks!' he said, laughing again.

I sighed helplessly. Two months with him and still I couldn't figure what feed reared such a breed.

'Anyway, even if your parents don't come to know, and you successfully go, let me tell you of my suicidal love. Your fickle snake won't be able to bear even the weight of dough.'

His extempore rhyme registered in the logical end. 'You mean the rope isn't strong enough?' I questioned, faintly aware of the answer.

'Tanie, for heavens get a grip. This is no direct to DVD Cinderella story.'

'Are you sure?' The urge to meet Rehaan was multiplying with every passing second. Where was he anyway? I got my answer a few minutes later. A bedlam of eerie noises in the otherwise still night revealed a black Skoda with its parking lights turned on. It pulled up a little before my gate, right in front of Sumer's.

'Prince Charming is here,' Sumer announced.

'I can see,' my reply was interjected by a nagging beep signalling call waiting. 'Sumer, hold,' I instructed and switched the call.

'Talking with?' I sensed impatience in his voice.

'Stuti,' I lied.

'Oh, why? Anyway, I am outside your house,' he said silkily.

'Yes, I can see your car,' I replied, trying to feel the silk.

'Where are you?'

'On the roof,' I replied.

'Alright, I'm waiting honey,' only his voice had the quality to paralyze me while my heartbeat escalated to unreachable heights.

'I'm on my way,' I announced, eager to experience more than just his voice.

'Should I get down?' he asked.

'No, don't,' I didn't want him to see Sumer, not now, not today. I disconnected the phone, resuming Sumer's call. 'Sumer, I hope I can count you on this,' I said, already knowing I could.

'Tanie, are you crazy? You'll fall down!' he spoke in a motherly, stern tone.

'I will, out of nervousness if you say that again,' I said, turning his warning into a feeble joke.

'Are you sure you're going?' he asked.

'Yes. Okay, I have to go now,' I spoke, waiting for his farewell.

'You cannot go. If you go, I will shout from the rooftop and I mean that literally.'

My heart sank. I saw Rehaan's car once again as Sumer continued with his implied warnings. I sighed in dejection; I had trusted him too early.

The fear of getting caught aggravates when known eyes see you, even worse, warn you. 'Bye Sumer,' I said and ran back inside, promising myself that I won't ever talk to him. I would delete him from my Facebook friend list, from Yahoo, from Skype and everywhere.

'Rehaan, I think Mom has got up,' I said, sitting on my bed. Lying to my boyfriend for the second time cracked the emotion dam further.

'Oh, what happened?' he was evidently disappointed.

'I am so sorry, I can hear Mom climb up the stairs. I'll call back in the morning.' I put down the phone, holding it long enough to switch off as the dam broke open and I tasted liquid salt coupled with bitterness that I had towards Sumer.

'I won't ever forgive him, even if Rehaan forgives me,' was

my last thought before sleep caught on me and the world outside rose to a fresh beginning.

'Tanie baby, rise for me. Mwuahahaha,' Sumer shook me back to the present: three months hence.

'I won't forgive you Sumer,' I mumbled my real dream's last line foolishly.

'God, how can someone sleep when I am driving and that also when you have just given a full-syllabus Maths test half an hour ago,' he grimaced.

'Are we home?' I asked with a faint laugh and strong rub on my eyes.

'Yes, if that confectioner seems homely enough,' he joked.

'Why have you stopped in the market?' I asked.

'Because,' his gaze shifted from my face, a little down, a little more. Full stop! 'Mom asked me to get some

M...I...L...K,' he said, pronouncing every letter of the last word.

'God, you are sick, Sumer!' I howled and pushed him out of the car. The giraffe, even after literally falling down on the cemented parking area, had his feet reach the edge of the seat.

'You want a lolly-dolly?' he asked, saucily playing with his zip.

'Get two small round toffees with it too,' I said stooping to his level.

'Hell Tanie! Only if Rehaan knew you were so sweetly sick,' he said and got up, brushing his ass and off he went into the shop.

❧

That sneak-out night, or shall I say 'early morning', I had decided to delete Sumer from my life had made me realize that everything does happen for the good.

Back then, I would have fulfilled my thoughts if he wouldn't have come knocking on my door at 6.30 in the morning.

I don't remember the reason he had cited to my mother who was forced out of bed on a Sunday. Must have been some superacademic lie about our weekly Maths test which was to start after two hours or she would have blasted us both.

That suddenly reminded me of the test results we had received today morning. Sumer had moved out early to fetch his car and I had taken his answer script for him.

All I remember about that Sunday long ago is his repetitive bang on my door while Mom made coffee for him and me, of me walking after much persuasion to the roof with my rope which I hadn't untied and then he climbing down the rope, struggling at every joint and miraculously falling only a few feet from above the ground.

It was then that I realized that he had risked his life just to prove he was concerned and not jealous. I was shocked; Mom was just surprised when she saw him enter again from the main door. 'But I went out just a few minutes ago,' he had said, taking advantage of Mom's sleep-deprived brain.

'Dreaming with open eyes?' Sumer said, throwing the milk tetrapack packet in my lap.

'By the way, I got your answer script for the test,' I said as we started to move again.

'How did Moochi (that's what we called our Maths teacher) check the test so fast?'

'Stuti said he was checking alongside as we submitted each sheet,' I answered, searching for his answer-script in my bag now. 'Here,' I said handing him his sheet.

'I am doomed!' Sumer's honest prediction boomed in the car. 'It's a freaking 25 on 100,' he exclaimed.

'It's just a weekly tuition test,' I tried to pacify him as the sudden increase in the speedometer had urged me to.

'Yeah, a weekly Maths full-syllabus test just a month before the pre-Boards begin,' he barked and honked to the poor three-wheeler let down by his machine's immobility.

'My pre-Boards don't start until December. You know, it's rather strange that our schools are both convents, are both neighbours, yet they can't coordinate exams,' I sighed.

'By the way, Tanie...sorry, I shouted at you,' he said softly.

'It's okay,' I shouted reassuringly.

We both laughed.

'Well, you know, you could take my answer-script and show it to your Mom. It's a 60, unlike your...whatever,' I said and laughed satanically.

It was rare when the near-perfect Sumer faltered and I wanted to leave no chance to glorify his fall.

'You bitch...,' he tried hard to mean it.

'You are too sweet to be my best friend, buddy,' I said, playing with the black Maggie noodles he carried around proudly.

He stopped the car in front of his house. I opened the door to step out.

'Tanie,' he spoke in a too-serious tone for the moment.

'Yes?' I asked, turning back to him and leaning on the door now.

'You actually meant that?' his eyes showed the faintest brush of moisture.

'Hell no, I am not giving my paper. Park and come over. We will decide something,' I replied, knowing our mothers won't be awake to welcome us. While his Dad was on ship, my Dad would be getting ready to putt and chip.

'Sure, okay,' he replied in return.

I turned around and took a step.

'Actually I was talking about the best-friend thing,' I heard a first time shy tone from behind.

I turned around and said, 'Yes, I mean every word of it... You truly are my best friend.'

I smiled, he smiled. All problems could wait.

※

'Good morning, Dad,' I wished Dad cheerfully, as he and his golf bag stood at the gate.

'Morning Tanie. Weren't you supposed to have a Maths test today morning?' he asked, looking confused.

'Yes, I just returned,' I said pointing to my bag.

'Oh,' he smiled a little embarrassedly.

'What Dad?' I demanded.

'Well, this top really suits you; didn't you wear it at some party last time?' he added a little carefully.

So this is where his apprehension got implanted. 'Dad, believe me, I still don't dress up as compared to the other girls there,' I informed him.

'How about sparing a Sunday?' he joked. It had the effect— my sweet, caring, almost friendly Dad had me laughing.

Still I refrained from telling him that I had especially straightened my hair today morning. Tuitions were more than studies, right? They were a medium to interact with the society (okay, just the boys).

'Good morning, uncle!' I heard Sumer's voice.

'Oh Sumer, good morning. Did you just get up? Then how did you commute, Tanie?' Dad asked him and then me.

'Dad,' I whined.

'What?' he responded.

'No uncle, don't worry. I just don't believe in ummm...'

'Taking a bath or getting ready,' I volunteered.

'Yes getting ready just for tuition,' he said.

'Okay kids, you enjoy. I am getting late,' he said and proceeded towards his car.

'Wait, I'll carry the golf set for you, uncle,' Sumer offered like a gentleman.

No no, Sumer. It's okay. Thank you,' Dad said and left. We walked back inside to my garden.

'Sumer...you suck,' I kicked him on his leg calf.

'Oh, that hurts Tanie,' he said, hopping on one leg.

'Don't dramatize. Okay, first you come to the tuition in your boxers.'

'Hell, they are Versace shorts,' he said, alarmed.

'Yeah, but they still look like boxers,' he gave me a dirty look. I turned a blind eye to it and continued, 'And then you have to act like a butler all the time!'

'Butler?' he asked confused. 'I'll carry it for you, uncle,' I tried my best to mimic his hoarse, deep voice.

'Tanie, you know what?'

I didn't respond.

'You are,' he said automatically.

'Did I ask you to answer?'

'Fine, I won't say a word now,' he said and took out his iPod and lay down on the grass.

'Fine...what is it?' my feminine instinct took over after a painful gap of two minutes.

'Talking to me?' he asked in a fake accent.

'*Haan kutte*, talking to you?' I felt like kicking him again.

'Nothing, I just had to say thank God, you aren't my girlfriend,' he said and closed his eyes, plugging his earplugs again. I bent down to unplug them.

'Wow, even Liaka likes Victoria Secret,' he said.

'Sumer!' I quickly retraced to my standing position. He just grinned like an idiot.

'Bye, I am going in and you are not invited,' I turned around.

'No please, don't. I am homeless, Tanie. Mom kicked me out,' he said in a pleading voice.

I turned around laughing. 'Are you serious?' Nothing in his world was serious though.

'Yes,' he said in a serious tone. I laughed loudly now.

'Are you okay? When I decide to joke, you get angry even before it starts and when I am serious, you laugh like there is no tomorrow,' I heard him and started laughing again. He changed his position and sat crosslegged now. 'What is wrong with you?' he demanded.

'Nothing,' I said and continued laughing.

'Tanie, if you laugh anymore, Rehaan will ummm..., you won't meet till next week.'

Something inside me immediately closed the laughter tap. I wasn't superstitious; it was just...love.

I sat down carefully on the grass and adjusted my top. While he smirked, I scowled and resumed, 'So what happened exactly?' I asked him.

'After I parked the car, I thought I'll keep the books inside and have my leftover pepperoni pizza and...'

'Haw, you had ordered pepperoni pizza last night? Without me?' I interjected and made a sad face.

'*Cholly*,' he said in a puppy voice.

'Anyway, continue,' I said, playing the hurt game.

'I said, I am *cholly baba*,' he said and held his ears. It was antics like this which made the giant look so cute.

'Okay, continue,' said I.

'Yeah, so where was I? Yes, pepperoni pizza. So I heated it and tip-toed to my room, so that Mom wouldn't wake up.'

'Yeah, so? If aunty didn't wake up, then...'

'Tan…Tan…let me finish, yaar,' he said and smiled at my reaction. 'Fine. No Tan…Tan; you are Tanie.'

'Better,' I said.

'*Haan* so, I went to my room and kept the answer-sheet on my study table. Suddenly I got the urge to do *susu*,' I wrinkled my nose at this again. 'Okay, pee, or urinate—whichever seems more civilized to you. So I went to the toilet and just when I had opened the button and then slowly unzipped and then even more slowly adjusted my boxer…'

'You are such a pervert,' I exclaimed. He was so obsessed with his manhood that he had to invariably get it in every conversation somehow.

'Yaar, I am not a pervert. First you only asked for details and then you say all this,' he tried his best to look offended.

'Okay, sorry.'

'Yeah! So, I had just started to pee, you know, the sensation of downpour after the minor drizzle.'

'Sum…'

'Okay, no lecture. Fine to cut it short, Mom came in the room, saw my paper and began with her, had-your-Dad-been-here lecture… and finally told me to just get lost.' He narrated the juiciest part in a jiffy. 'So what should I do now?' he asked.

'Right now, come inside. I am hungry,' I said and got up.

'Me too,' he said, extending his arm. And I called him a gentleman some time back.

'C'mon,' I extended my hand and can you guess what happened next? If you thought he pulled me towards himself you are wrong. He would have done that only if food wasn't involved. Bloody hypocrite! Hungry, homeless giant!

We started walking towards the drawing-room door.

'Tanie?'

'Hmm…?'

'You hate it when I talk about my...'

'Yes, Sumer,' I cut him.

'Okay...I am sorry.'

'No, yaar, don't get senti again. It's okay, *pucca*.'

'It is?'

'Yeah.'

'Okay, so did I tell you about this incident, last week?'

'No.'

'Okay, here it goes. I went to shop. In the Benetton changing room, just when I had unzipped...'

'Sumer!'

I hopelessly laughed, he hopefully laughed, problem solved.

13

So-Kool Buddies

July

When neighbour starts going to my neighbouring school.

'And the Oscar for the strongest oxymoron of the year goes to holiday homework,' I lazily said into my cell phone.

'Was that supposed to make me laugh?' Stuti questioned. We laughed anyway.

'But seriously Stuti, you pick up any dictionary and find the meanings. 'Holiday' means, 'recreation, festivity where no work is done' and 'homework'—a word featuring on the next page is—'work done at home'. Huh, so much for contra...' A yawn stopped me from completing the 'dictions'.

'Dickson's?' she asked confused.

'I said contradictions not di...anyway, that's what I can expect from you at 3 a.m.,' I joked.

'What! It's three already?'

We had been talking for, according to my cell phone screen, forty-five minutes and as I write, fourteen seconds.

'No, it's three one now,' I said seriously and we both laughed.

'So, what is exactly left in your holiday homework now and

this time answer my question first?' Stuti said and we laughed again.

'Okay, I am just left with Hindi,' I informed her.

'Bitch! I thought you were not doing Maths too. Now tomorrow...I mean today,' we laughed again. 'I will have to stand alone outside the class.'

'I didn't do it; I got Hindi and Maths outsourced,' I informed and we both laughed again.

'So you got the model on volume of cone and cylinder made from outside...it must have come out pretty well,' she remarked.

I adjusted myself, so I could see the model from the bed. 'From here the cone looks like a...like a Dildo,' I said and we both laughed again.

'Don't worry. Renuka ma'am won't let it go waste,' Stuti said and we laughed to the power of n.

'So how is Rehaan *jiju*?' Stuti asked after some time.

'Should be fine,' I replied a little too casually.

'Fought again?'

My silence gave away the answer.

'Reason?' she demanded.

'Nothing,' I said, trying to avoid the topic.

'Go on.' Stuti would let me do everything but that.

'Okay, it's kind of silly but still...' I warned.

'It can't be sillier than your last "little" fight, can it?' she asked and we both laughed again.

The last time we had fought was because Rehaan had addressed me as 'my little baby'. Agreed he is two years elder and six inches taller and calls me 'baby' all the time but the word 'little' itself made me so little. And then we had argued or rather I had started replying him blandly and on his repeated asking about what was wrong, I had just said, 'Little baby doesn't know how to answer.'

'Tanie, there...' Stuti's voice brought me back from the memory.

'Yeah, sorry. Was just thinking...I think...' I said sheepishly. We both laughed briefly.

'So?' Stuti said.

'So, nothing Stuti. It wasn't exactly a fight either. It was just that before you called, like at 12.30 or something, he had called and we talked generally about how our respective day had been.'

'So where does exactly the fight feature?' she asked impatiently. The gossip girl avatar was overpowering her.

'Yaar, we talked around till 2 a.m., I think and then he had to go to sleep. He had tuitions at 6 a.m. and all. He wished me goodnight and everything. So at 2, he said goodbye and asked me to disconnect the call. But I refused. It's me who always hangs up on him. This time I just didn't want to,' I said feebly.

'Hmmm...,' Stuti's voice conveyed that she knew where we were getting at.

'And then I told him to cut the call and he didn't. The same reason—a gentleman never hangs up on a young beautiful girl. But I told him this time..."Just do it", but still he didn't agree and after continuously requesting him, I got a bit irritated and told him that I'd let him stay on hold for the whole night. And he said, 'Fine' and I said, 'Fine' and then you called...,' I narrated the whole situation concisely.

'So you hung on him finally?' Stuti aimed a question-cum-statement.

'Actually, he is still on hold,' I said slowly.

'God, Tanie! His top up will end. You are such an expensive girlfriend,' she sighed and we both laughed again.

Stuti and I were awarded the 'Laughing Friends' title in Class VII. Three years later, we could proudly proclaim that we not only lived up, rather gave a whole new dimension to it. It took enormous effort on our part to maintain our hat-trick, for it isn't easy to laugh at any and every situation, nor is it easy to flex your jaws all the time when anything remotely related to humour comes up. We loved to laugh with a group and then laugh at the group. 'Snobby hobby', but we loved it and still do.

'So how is your neighbour?' Stuti asked suddenly. 'He has a name, Stuti,' I replied.

'Somebody is getting possessive,' Stuti joked.

I decided to ignore it. 'Even he is starting school tomorrow; I mean today.'

We laughed again. I told you we laugh to kill.

'He is pretty tall yaar...is he long too?'

'Chii...,' I replied and we laughed again.

My best friend had met my new best friend twice in June, when she had come over to spend a day. Moreover because of M-2-Mt (Mummy-to-Mummy talk), Aarti aunty had made him join the same Maths and Science tuitions we used to go to. Sumer and I carpooled most of the time.

'He has a girlfriend Stuti and I have seen her pictures. She is beautiful,' I said teasingly.

'So what, Tanie? Let him be a player—she there, you here,'

'Stuti!' I was too shocked to say anything else.

'Kidding, yaar.'

We both laughed again. 'So has Rehaan met him?'

'No, they haven't met till now. Just seen each other,' I informed her.

'And he is okay with you both walking together every evening and you going over to his place?' she had come back to her 'gossip girl *avatar*'.

'Well, my parents know his parents well. They don't have a problem, I know he is decent, so there isn't a problem,' I said in a matter-of-fact tone.

Stuti yawned.

'Huh, that was honest,' I protested.

'Did I say anything? Is it guilty conscience?' She questioned and we laughed.

'Not even a bit,' I said.

'That's good, okay. I better go to sleep now. It's kind of late.'

'Hmmm yes,' I looked at the wall clock '4 a.m. is definitely late.'

We both laughed for some time, wished each other good night and I put down the receiver and got up to switch off the night lamp. I returned to my bed after two minutes and smiled for the last time before sleeping, on looking at a certain name flashing on my screen. The gentleman still hadn't disconnected my call.

🐾

'I have always wanted to do this,' he says, looking into my eyes.

'Over here?' I question, even though the brain waves have been converted to audible reception after a light year. 'Yes, it has always been my dream to have you in my life, to be with you, to want you to be the one who wakes me up every morning in bed,' he replies now tracing my lips.

My physical frame reacts strongly to this electric touch.

'Don't worry, I won't hurt you,' he assures me. I don't fear his touch; every trace his hand makes, leaves a newly sketched me.

A 'me' who is overpowered just by his shadow and when this portal of perfection is there to see, to touch, to feel, to believe, the new 'me' is abound with oozing emotions liquefied and quantified in action. Now he moves his hand and wipes off the single liquid emotion that has found birth in the eye and would attain nirvana in my heart.

His heavy breathing reminds me that he is for real.

Suddenly he holds my waist and I get clouded by dizziness and a feeling of ecstasy. I hear him say something; his voice can melt the sun while the intensity of his gaze can blast it. I also hear the exhaust fan; today its noise is the most pleasant music my eardrums have ever been vibrated with. He makes me sit on the pot. Yes, for some strange reason we are in my bathroom.

He walks over to the sink and picks up my toothbrush and paste. He wants it to be perfect, I smile.

'Brush your teeth,' he says holding out the toothbrush which is smeared with a thin line of toothpaste squeezed and pressed gently from its tube. He helps me do the gargle, cupping his hand to feed me with water.

My cheeks burn, so does the desire to fix his hands to my lips. He wets a face towel next and wipes it very slowly on my face. I let him get familiar with the eyes that only want to see him, the nose that has a special nostril dedicated to his fragrance, the lips which want to taste his, the cheeks which want his imprint.

'You are almost ready,' he says mystically.

I let him guide me; I let him empower me; I let him come closer to my soul, to my physical being as I sit on the pot. He is now sitting in the Indian style, his arms resting on my thighs. I am an electric pole and he the meter. His face inches forward. My eyes close and...

'Tanie, are you sleeping inside? The driver is waiting!' Mom shouted, her barbarous banging having the same volume and strength.

'Tanieee!' I heard Mom repeat my name again.

'Yes, two minutes,' I tried my best to shout back.

I looked around—the pot, the exhaust fan, the toothpaste tube without the lid, the fallen toothbrush and an overflowing shower tub. 'Since how long have I been dreaming?' I wondered and smiled. The dream had left an impact—a sticky, satisfied one.

I was late for school. After quickly throwing the holiday

homework bag and keeping the Maths model carefully in the empty class, I headed towards the auditorium for assembly and reached precisely just when the 'Our Father Who Art...' started.

Taking advantage of the closed eyes of those who kept an eye, I quickly joined my class line. 'Phew, saved from another late stamp,' I muttered slowly.

The assembly, even after two months of vacation, defined what monotony is in terms of practicality. The ten minutes-longer-than long assembly had all the ingredients of a stale cake and the cherry on the icing this time was the special warning to Class X, the mention of the 'B' word.

Throughout the assembly I kept looking out for Stuti or Megha...but unsuccessfully.

'Hey Saachi, how were hols? Where is Stuti?' I asked my parallel partner as soon as the head girl ended her squeaky voiced 'school disperse'.

'Oh hi, Tanie! Late on the first day of school after vacation? Difficult, isn't it, to get up so early and this skirt?'

'Yeah, I know. Have you seen Stuti or Megha?' I interjected before she could begin describing the woes everyone obviously felt but didn't need to discuss.

'I saw Megha's bag in the class; no idea about Stuti,' she flashed an apologetic smile.

I thanked her and got out of the line which was moving towards our classroom.

'Tanie, get back into line,' screamed the class monitor, the nerd, Queen Surbhi.

'I need to go to the washroom,' I lied and started walking towards the washroom which was at the opposite end of the corridor and viola! I found her there, her bag kept on the marble slab holding the sink and the Science model on one side.

'Hey, got late. No option. My diary page is already full with late stamps,' she said and we laughed. 'So, you came looking for me?' she asked next.

'Kind of. Actually I had this dream today morning,' and I began describing all that I had seen.

'What you had was a wet dream.' Stuti concluded and before we could laugh, the door opened.

'Hello, my bathroom beauties.' It was Megha. 'Saachi told me you are here,' she said and hugged me and then Stuti.

Megha was the tip of our trio—the tip not because she had the sharpest features, a slender frame, high-pointed cheekbones and long rebonded hair or not because she had loads and loads of money and owned two of the coolest restaurants in the city, even not because she had a personal driver and Mercedes to drive her around and definitely not because of her long lists of admirers in the neighbouring school and the city. She was the tip because she was always a step higher than us, courtesy the already-listed points above.

'How was London and the cruise?' I asked her.

'Oh great...shopped till I dropped,' she dramatized a faint and Stuti giggled.

Megha was closer to me than she was to Stuti—another reason for the tip.

'So, what are we exactly doing here?' I asked them.

'Let's go to class; the zero period will end soon,' Stuti said.

'Oh my God, my skirt is till my knees,' Megha shrieked, looking at herself in the mirror and her hands responded to the disaster quickly by unbuckling her belt and opening her skirt hooks. Folds in the clockwise direction, once in the anti, hook them up before buckling and chuckling. Hence we present you the modern convent-going girl whose hair is (not) always plaited, whose shirt buttons are (not) always fastened to the peak of suffocation, whose lips are (not) always missing the gloss and the sunshine radiance, whose ears are (not) always bare, a little sparkle and shine. C'mon sisters, there's nothing to mind.

'Help me carry this,' Stuti's finger pointed towards her model.

'Yeah,' my reply was drained in the sound indicating the commencement of the first period.

'Fuck, Dhanno will kill us…quick,' Megha said and opened the door while Stuti and I followed.

We started jogging towards our class. A few steps before, we halted and resumed the casual *I-don't-care-about-the-rules walk*. Girls looked up to us. We had a reputation to maintain right!

'By the way Tanie, what do you have to say about a certain "S" factor in your life?' Megha asked, just as we were about to enter the class.

"S" factor?' I asked, confused.

We reached the door. Dhanno aka Dhanvantri Verma was taking the attendance, hence the silence in the class stung.

Stuti banged the door loudly. Everyone giggled. Dhanno looked up from her desk. 'How predictable,' she said aloud. Stuti gave an innocent look.

'May we come in, ma'am?' Megha asked for us.

Ms Dhanvantri Verma, our poised (not), young (not), married (not), English-cum-class-teacher-cum-Oscar-winning-disciplinarian-cum-the-undisputed queen of the title of the deadliest, obnoxious and monotonous teacher asked me and Stuti to stop at the door while Megha went and occupied her seat. Third row, second last bench.

'So Stuti, I didn't see you in the assembly and why are you coming with your bag now and Tanie, I presume you came in late too' she accused us, adjusting her spectacles.

'Yes ma'am, you are right,' Stuti spoke on our behalf—her

mind-mill had definitely started churning a new excuse.

'And why?' she asked, raising her tone.

'Actually ma'am, it's kind of personal,' Stuti said to my surprise.

'And what is it?' she asked.

'Ma'am, if I announce it in front of everybody, how would it remain personal?' Stuti said slowly and the whole class laughed. I fought against my reflexes to suppress a grin.

'Silence!' she said loudly. 'You don't have to be cheeky the first thing in the morning,' she said in a harsh tone.

'Sorry, ma'am,' I said on Stuti's behalf.

'Why are you sorry?' she asked.

'Ma'am, actually I reached school on time...but instead of going to class, I went to the washroom straightaway,' Stuti said.

'Why?' she asked.

'Actually ma'am, this time of the month isn't...,' Stuti paused and continued in a low voice 'the best time of the month for me.' The class and I tried hard to control our laughter after looking at her embarrassed plus alarmed face.

Stuti nudged me from behind. I understood my cue and began, 'And ma'am, since I had an extra, you know...the thing, I went to the washroom to help her out and got late in the process.'

'Well summed up,' Stuti whispered into my ear.

'Sit,' she said in a surprisingly low voice and we proceeded to take our seats.

❧

'Now that was an epic excuse,' Megha congratulated me as I took the seat next to her while Stuti came and sat behind us with Saachi.

'How many periods do I have with you today?' Dhanno

asked and a unanimous giggle engulfed the class. 'What's the joke?' she demanded.

Nobody replied.

She grumbled something about manners and asked us to take out our holiday homework.

🐿

'So you still haven't told me about the "S" factor,' Megha wrote on the shared Science book on our desk during the fourth period.

'What "S" factor?' I wrote back as the teacher explained something about carbon compounds.

'SUMER SINGH DHILLON,' she wrote in big, bold letters.

'Bitch, you spoiled my Science book!' I wrote again, not realizing I was spoiling it further.

She grinned at me. 'So?' she wrote in small letters on the little white space in the margin. I added a 'what' to it.

'Nothing. Will talk in break,' she wrote and turned her attention towards the blackboard.

'Sumer is my new neighbour, Megha,' I informed as soon as the bell rang for recess.

'So, why is he all over your Facebook page?' she questioned like a prying reporter questions a celebrity.

'Well...he has been around for the past two months, the two months when you weren't here and umm...he is in our neighbouring school and what else? Yes, my Mom and his Mom have become the best of friends. We both take Liaka for a walk every evening and yeah, he comes for the same Science and Maths tuition. So, you would see him pretty soon,' I said and got up.

'Oh...has Rehaan met him?' she asked, also getting up.

'Can you please continue this little interview in the canteen?' Stuti shouted from the door.

'Sure,' we both replied in unison and started walking towards the door.

'So, Rehaan hasn't met him?' Megha spoke automatically in the canteen, a few minutes later.

'He hasn't...just seen him,' I said, taking a sip from the coke can.

'And he is cool, with you both walking and talking?' she asked, holding her fork full of oily noodles hanging in mid air.

'Yes. Why would he have a problem? And why are you asking the same questions that Stuti asked me last night?' I asked her.

'Your neighbour seems to be pretty cute actually,' she said and smiled.

It may surprise you, but Megha had been single since the past two months.

'He's taken Megha,' Stuti said, snatching my coke can.
'Courtesy,' I reminded her slowly.

'What's that?' she asked.

'Stop it both of you...so, he's taken by whom?' Megha asked interestedly.

'A *girl* called Liaka...' Megha smiled.

'Yes, he knows my bitch's name is Liaka as well,' she smiled some more.

'And in any case, Megha darling,' Stuti interjected seductively, 'I already have my eyes on him.' We all laughed.

'If Sumer came to know that both my best friends find him cute...he'd reach the zenith of narcissism,' I said, as we heard the bell ring and started walking back for four more periods of mental torture.

❦

'Hey Sumer!' I shouted and asked my driver to stop the car in front of his gate.

'Hey,' came the reply.

I got down from the car. Aarti aunty was parking her Civic in the driveway.

'So, how was your first day in school?' I asked him excitedly.

'It was fine...am not really used to an all-boys environment actually...but otherwise it went off well,' he said, playing with his curly hair.

'Sounds good...were you ragged or something?'

'Nope. In fact, I am already selected for some interschool debate,' he said casually.

'That's great.'

'Hello, *beta*!' Aarti aunty's greeting wasn't overflowing with enthusiasm today.

'Hello, aunty,' I said, after she reached the gate.

'Your uniform reminds me of my school days,' she said, holding my hands.

'Why Mom...did you also wear such hideous skirts?' he asked and laughed while we both gave him a dirty look.

'Ignore him, *beta*,' Aarti aunty said weakly.

'Aunty, you look a bit tired,' I observed.

'She was having a tough time driving,' Sumer replied for her.

'If we don't find a driver soon, Sumer will have to join the school bus.'

He made a disgusting face at this suggestion. How like me, I thought.

'Hey Tanie, how do you commute to school?' he asked with a sudden interest.

'In the morning Dad drops me and in the afternoon generally, the driver or Dad,' I informed him.

'Then let's carpool for school too...our schools begin almost at the same time anyway,' he said excitedly.

'I won't mind if you can risk getting late every day by a

couple of minutes,' I said and smiled.

'I'm no morning person either,' he said.

'So Mom, isn't it a cool idea?' he asked Aunty casually.

'Maybe.. .your father also had to go back to sail just a week before your school began,' she said in a complaining tone.

'Oh Mom, c'mon, don't start it all over again,' Sumer protested.

'Okay *beta*, I'll talk to Smiley about this today evening,' she said and asked us both to come inside.

'No aunty, I'd rather go now. Mom must be anxious...Bye aunty... Bye Sumer. I'll meet you in the evening,' I said and walked back to my car.

🐾

'I am so sorry, uncle,' were Sumer's first words after he sat in the car the next morning.

'And I thought only I had a problem getting up early,' I said jokingly.

'I am sorry, uncle,' Sumer said again.

'Just be careful next time...Tanie herself has got a diary full of late stamps.'

'Dad!' I protested. He ignored it and started talking to Sumer about his alma mater and Sumer's present school.

'Drive faster Dad, it's already 7.55 a.m.,' I reminded him after a few minutes.

'What time does your school start?' Dad asked Sumer.

'At 8,' I answered for him.

Dad gave a sly look. 'You seem to know a lot about your neighbouring school?' he commented.

'Stuti's younger brother studies there, Dad!' I said, trying to hide the obvious.

We reached Sumer's school first. 'Uncle, you can drop me

at the gate itself,' Sumer said.

'No...no...it's okay,' Dad said, turning his car inside. Yes, just what I wanted, I thought. Now I would get a chance to go to his school (even if it's just the parking area) every day. Dad stopped the car in the parking area.

'Thank you,' he said and got down, while I was too busy checking out the known and the unknown guys.

৺

'So you will carpool every day?' Megha asked me.

We were walking to the parking lot after the eighth period ended. Stuti was absent today for reasons best known to her.

'Yup! In fact, the driver was supposed to pick him up first,' I said playing up to Megha's excitement.

'Does that mean he will be there in the car just now?' Megha was definitely getting excited.

'Yup! Hey, I can see your car. Okay, bye Megha,' I said as soon as we reached the parking lot.

'No!' she said loudly.

I started to laugh.

'What?' she demanded.

'Nothing. Come along. Won't you walk me to my car?' I said and smiled.

'Yes,' she said with a twinkle in her eye.

Sumer didn't even know that perhaps the hottest girl in school was especially coming to meet him. Lucky bastard! Any guy endowed with natural hormones would die to be in his place.

We searched for my car but couldn't find it.

'There,' Megha pointed out to a white Skoda, as it entered the gate.

Two minutes later the car came and halted just near us.

Sumer was sitting in the front passenger seat. I signalled him to get down. He opened the door.

'*Ajay bhaiya, side per park kar lo,*' I told my driver.

The first thing that I also think Megha noticed about him was his originally supposed to be high, but in his case, low-waist school pants. The pull of gravity had its effects after all. His white shirt was tucked out and his belt was hanging around his neck.

'Hey Tanie and umm...Tanie *ki* friend,' he greeted me and Megha confidently.

This guy had balls for sure. Generally guys stammer when they stand in front of Megha.

'Hey,' I replied, while Megha just smiled. She had begun with her Miss Attitude role.

'So this is how Holy Heart Convent looks like,' Sumer said, extending his arms in a weird action.

'What are you doing?' I hissed.

'No man, but seriously, this classmate of mine...he saw me getting down from your car today morning and the first thing he says is, *"Arre tu Tanie ka bhai hai?"*

We both smiled. He still didn't know that he had befriended the girls.

'And you won't believe it, but when I told him and the other guys who had crowded around us that I am your neighbour, they got all the more excited.' I couldn't help but blush. 'I didn't know you are so famous yaar...so now, I actually know why guys were getting friendly with me today.'

'Well, then, you should thank your stars you have me as your neighbour,' I said proudly.

Megha nudged me from behind. 'Sorry,' she said, trying to pass off the nudge as an accident.

I began, 'Sumer this is...'

He interrupted, 'But they were telling me about this friend of yours...what's her name...*haan*, Megha...'

'Sum...,' I tried to stop him but he wouldn't.

'Yeah, they were like *woh toh tota hai ekdum, chicken tangri.*'

Great there goes his leftover chance. I looked at Megha, who surprisingly seemed to portray no sign of being uncomfortable.

'Hi, I am Megha,' she suddenly spoke.

'Oh, h...h...hi!' he said with the shock in his voice evident.

'And what other dish am I exactly?' Megha asked in good humour.

'Ummm...I am sorry yaar...I didn't know,' he began, his face revealing the embarrassment.

'It's okay. Chill,' Megha said and we all laughed.

'Okay, I'll make a move now. My driver is waiting,' Megha informed and bid us 'bye'.

'By the way Megha,' Sumer suddenly said. 'Hmm...?' she asked.

'I think my classmates were wrong...you are more of a *malia kebab*,' he said and laughed.

'Sumer!' I nudged him and laughed hopelessly.

'I'll remember,' Megha said and walked back smiling to her car.

I laughed, he laughed, problem solved.

14

Back-up Buddies and the Surprise

Tanie

1 August

'Hello, who is this?' I carefully asked, picking up an unknown call at 11.45 p.m.

'It's me,' I heard a strange whisper in reply.

'Rehaan.... *jaan*, is that you? Don't fool around, baby.'

'No Tanie Brar, I am not your baby...I know you very well but you don't know me...I know you bunked your Science tuition two days ago for a date with your *jaan*,' the hoarse whisper continued.

'Shut up, Stuti!'

'Isn't Stuti already shut up? She is sleeping till 12 o'clock, I believe.'

'Oh Maggie, it's you. Where's your private number?' I asked, feeling a bit relieved.

'I am no Maggie noodles...nor am I your friend Megha.'

I thought of calling Rehaan from the landline.

'What are you thinking of calling Rehaan from? Your landline?'

An instant balloon of fear burst inside my body. 'Who is this?' I asked, mustering all the courage that was left.

'*Tan-tanna-tan-tan-tan-taara, bajne waale hai barah.*' I heard a familiar, definitely-not-musical voice this time.

'Fuck you, Sumer!' I shouted into the phone as the tension went into the past tense.

'Sorry *tan-tan*...but you sounded so constipated,' he said and laughed.

'I should have guessed that it'll be you only, *saala* donkey.'

'Well, I thought you'd realize sooner...You took everyone's name except mine.

'So what's up?' I asked, jumping on to my bed.

'Nothing...waiting for minutes to midnight. This is my new number by the way,' he said.

'Yeah. So, what is my gift for Friendship Day,' I asked jokingly.

'Well there is something grand for sure...'

'Hmmm...a surprise! Not bad, not bad. So what time is everyone coming tomorrow?' I asked.

'Twelve thirtyish...'

'Okay, I'll come early then. You would need help with the furniture and stuff.'

'Sure, so are Megha and Stuti's parents cool about hanging out at my place?'

'I don't think so,' I replied gravely.

'So they aren't coming?' the disappointment in his voice rose.

'They are, dude. Chill...According to their parents, they are spending the day at my place.'

'Oh, okay,' he said, relieved.

'By the way, why are you so keen to invite them to your room?' I teased.

'Nothing yaar, I thought my school friends and you people

could together have fun in a group.'

I laughed loudly.

'What?' he demanded.

'Nothing.'

'Oh Tanie, you are so sick,' he grimaced and laughed. 'But yeah, I really won't mind Megha in my room with me,' he said saucily.

'Bloody flirt! I think I need to call Liaka,' I said and laughed.

'Who Liaka? Doesn't she sleep in your room only?' he asked.

'Sumer, I meant your Liaka.'

'Oh, sorry.'

He laughed, I laughed, problem solved.

❧

The next morning—Friendship Day.

I pressed Sumer's bell, I mean, his doorbell and seconds later Aarti aunty opened the door.

'Tanieee, good morning. Come on in!' Her over-excessive enthusiasm was routine now. 'So, what are you people up to now?' she questioned, as she guided me to the living room.

'Nothing much, aunty, just thought of setting up his room and…stuff.'

We sat down on the king-size sofas.

'So, who all are coming?' she asked, keeping her feet on the sofa.

'I think Stuti (my best, his good friend), Megha (my best, his 'close' friend), Kabir (his best, Stuti's 'just friend'), Siddhartha (his good friend, my not-so-good friend and Megha's once upon a time 'special' friend) and I don't know if he has invited anyone else too,' I answered.

'Sumer just won't listen,' she sighed. I suppressed a grin. It was characteristic of mothers to complain about their stubborn teenaged offspring in front of their equally stubborn friends. She continued, 'I told him that I would get his room painted but he just won't listen...all these self-spray paintings and graffiti and what not,' she mouthed our plans like they were ill omens. 'He is only in control when his father is around.'

'And you too,' I wanted to say. 'I don't know, aunty,' I said instead.

'Your generation just wants freedom and space.' *And you give everything except that*, I spoke in my head and smiled on.

Suddenly aunty called out to the maid, *'Didi ke liye coke.'*

My smile increased. Aerated drinks were repulsive ingredients in my mother's grocery list.

'So when will uncle be back from sail?' I asked out of politeness. The lady had just offered me a pious liquid, after all.

'By Christmas. He is not taking leave before so that he can be here till Sumer's Board exams.'

Gr...r...r...eat, there goes my Sunday, the bombastic 'B' word.

'Sumer is still sleeping, I think,' aunty said, after two minutes.

'Huh, sleeping?' I checked my watch. It was 11.30 a.m. 'I'll go and wake him up,' I said, getting up. 'No!' aunty got up in a swift reflex move. 'I'll call him.' I sat down again, while aunty retrieved her mobile from her jeans pocket. 'Speed dial, that's how I wake him up for school. He needs to be called every ten minutes,' she explained. I smiled. Seriously, given a choice, he would choose sleep over sex.

'Hello Sumer...not afternoon, it's morning *beta*.' I giggled as aunty went on, 'No, your father hasn't called. Sumer, I think you had plans for today.'

'Oh fuck!' Did I just hear Sumer shout out 'fuck' to his Mom on the phone?

Aunty came to my rescue with the answer, 'Sumer Singh Dhillon, behave!' Her shout was loud enough to reach upstairs anyway. She put down the phone and looked at me. 'Sorry Tanie, but this boy sometimes is just...'

'Like a boy,' I suggested and we both laughed a feminist laugh.

'So, what was Mom doing?' she asked, sitting back again.

'Getting the house cleaned...I think.' Isn't that what mothers do all day long anyway?

'Oh okay. There is hardly anything to get cleaned here... just the two of us now,' aunty offered, as if she was guilty of not adhering to the first clause of the charter of the housewife clan's constitution: *Clean like a mean machine.*

Coke was served and the next second, a boy in blue Scooby Doo boxers and an oversized Mickey Mouse T-shirt came into sight. 'Why have you come so early?' his groggy voice echoed as he descended the steps.

He came and sat on the armrest of the sofa occupied by aunty. 'How rude of you!' aunty exclaimed.

'Oh Mom, I just meant, weren't you supposed to come later?' he said and bent forward to pick up my coke glass and take a sip.

Aunty snatched the glass from him and suddenly slapped his bare thigh hard. 'At least dress up properly.'

He rubbed his hairy thigh and asked, 'Why?' He got up and started walking towards the kitchen. 'Will you have something?'

A fan and a rope. 'Nothing,' I said.

He slammed the fridge door shut and walked back with a carton of Nestle milk. 'Take a glass at least and go. Get dressed,' aunty ordered in a pleading tone. He ignored it.

'Tanie, tell me, am I naked or what? Or do I make you uncomfortable?'

Spotlight, I so need a rope now to strangle a boxer-wearing boy. 'Just get ready. Everyone would be coming soon,' I said trying hard to look shy and embarrassed.

'All the more better. The girls are coming, *naa.*'

'S...U...M...E...R,' his cool Mom lost her cool; well literally. He dashed upstairs. 'This boy is just not scared of me...he thinks I am his...'

'Yo, Mamma,' we heard him shout.

I laughed here, he laughed there, problem solved.

⁂

'Hey...not bad yaar, the room looks so...'

'Naked?' a pyjama-wearing boy suggested and smiled.

I had come early to help him empty his sparsely furnished room but the honeymoon bouncing, thick eleven-inch, without-a-frame mattress he called bed was already shifted to one corner. So were the study table and the movable cupboard. All of them were covered with dark bed sheets.

'I was awake till 2 a.m. to get this done,' he said and rubbed his eyes. I couldn't help but smile at his sweetness.

'Where is the LCD?' I inquired.

'Took it off, don't want to spoil it,' he said responsibly.

'It wasn't outside in the lobby... Where is it?' I observed and questioned.

'Umm...in the toilet.' I stood there transfixed at his intellectual dumbness.

'What?' he gave me a dirty look.

'You don't want to spoil it? Dude! Water, electricity, metal, Physics...God!' I paused between each concept and simultaneously took a step towards his toilet.

'Tanie, wait.' I turned around to his shout and my foot hit upon an extra-large polythene bag. I bent down and picked it up.

'Blue suits you,' he smirked. FUCK blue, my underwear colour; Fuck Sumer, fuck you. I instantly got up and threw the plastic bag at him. He dodged it and the plastic bag fell.

'Oh my God!' he actually howled.

'What?' I asked, wondering if the not-so-heavy plastic bag had hit him hard on a soft point.

'Nothing,' he picked up the plastic bag and hugged it passionately. Before I could question him further on his plastic romance, his phone rang. 'Yes Mom...okay, coming in a second,' he ended the call. 'I'll be back in two minutes. The spray cans are in that box,' he said and went out of his room, taking the bag along.

He returned five minutes later. 'So what's there in that bag?' I was intrigued beyond control.

'Nothing,' he said and checked the time, '12.20 p.m. they should be here soon.'

'So, what's in the bag?' I demanded, hands on hips.

'Nothing *tan-tan*,' he smiled awkwardly. I gave him the look.

'Nothing *na*,' he said, a little paranoid. I knew it was time to use the last weapon.

'Hmmm...if you don't want to tell, it's okay.'

'Thanks,' he quickly responded.

'But I thought we were best friends and don't best friends share everything—secrets...and that too on Friendship Day.' I said in a low voice and bated the forcefully liquefied eyes. The weapon hit the bull's eye, aka his heart.

'Oh Tanie...' his tone said it all. 'Okay, promise you won't tell this to anyone,' he said apprehensively.

'So what's in the bag?' my low tone instantly reached an exciting high. *'Men are emotional fools,'* I repeated in my mind and smiled silently.

'Okay, I'll just be back,' he walked out of the room and

returned with two bean bags.

'Yes?' I asked after we were seated.

He undid the knot and took out a handful of small zip-lock packets and passed them over to me. I examined one of the zip locks.

'Used ice cream sticks?'

'Liaka and I shared it for the first time,' a soft voice replied. A tsunami of emotions rose inside me. My voice swelled and cracked. This guy was really in love. I reached out for his hand and pressed it lightly.

'That is so sweet, yaar,' I managed to mumble.

'Yeah, I know, even though she paid for it.' A smile graced my face as a tear bungee jumped from my eye. 'Idiot,' I wiped my eye and proceeded to the next zip lock—a pen.

'Hmmm...let me guess. She gave it to you some day in class or something.'

He smiled sheepishly.

'Thought so,' I said.

'Actually this was her favourite pen.'

'Was?' I asked.

'Till the day I stole it from her pencil box.'

I laughed out loud now. 'Why did you steal it?'

'So that I could return it like Superman,' he said, extending his arm in the Superman style.

'So why didn't you?' I asked, confused.

'We started going out before that only...and it is a pretty expensive pen too, yaar.' I laughed out louder now.

'And what is this—a hair clip? Hmmm...explain.'

'Oh this?' The smile on his face increased with each passing second. 'This little clip got me suspended for a week.'

'How?' I clapped my hands in excitement.

'Hmmm...I think it was the History period and Liaka was

playing with my hair when the principal saw us through the window or something. He stormed in, took us both to his office and confiscated the clip.'

'But you have it now,' I reasoned.

'Yeah,' his eyes had a mischievous gleam. 'In the office, Liaka profusely apologized, but all I did was fold my hands and ask for the clip, instead of rendering an apology,' he coughed. 'The principal threw the clip at me and the rest, as they say, is history.'

'Aww, how heroic! You must have felt so proud,' I began.

'Not really. Dad was at home at that time,' our smiles faded momentarily, only to give birth to a deafening laugh. His phone rang again and he picked it up, laughing, 'Hullo, Oh hi, Re... Resham! Yeah dude...alright...in a minute,' he got up from the bean bag. I looked at him, puzzled.

'School friend...has come to give some notes,' he offered.

'I'll come along,' I said, getting up.

'No...no, you stay. Call and ask Stuti and Megha. You will have to go to your house to get them too.'

'Hmm...okay,' I complied as my eyes rested on the remaining zip locks. 'Surely,' I side smiled. 'Just get me a coke,' I said, before he closed the door.

I was busy imagining the history behind the tissue paper in one zip lock when my phone buzzed. 'Sumer?' I asked in surprise.

'Tanie, I think you forgot about the surprise,' he said silkily.

'Oh yes, the surprise,' I said aloud. I honestly had forgotten about it.

'Well, close your eyes then tan-tan,' he instructed.

'Sumer, where are you?' I got up from the bean bag to walk out.

'Hey, stay in the room...okay,' he said.

'Fine,' I replied.

'Okay, close your eyes,' he repeated.

'I already have,' I lied.

'You haven't,' he said.

'Hey...can you see me?' I said, looking all around.

'No, but I know,' he said and disconnected the call. The next second, the door opened.

'Surprise!' Sumer shouted and behind him walked in the love of my life...Rehaan.

❦

'Oh, my God! I love you,' I shrieked and ran forward to hug him while the other male stood there, open-armed. Oops...I forgot to mention that the 'him' here was not Rehaan but Sumer. I realized my mistake as soon as Sumer whispered in my ear, 'Hug Rehaan first, idiot.'

I instantly let go of Sumer and looked at Rehaan. Honestly he looked pretty confused standing there with open arms and an open mouth.

'I love you too, Rehaan,' I hugged him tightly, not giving him a chance to speak.

'Ummm...I know the bed is not in its original place, but it's still usable, I think,' Sumer said slowly after two minutes. We instantly broke the embrace. I grinned like an idiot while Rehaan just smiled, a little embarrassed.

'So, like my surprise?' Sumer asked me.

I looked at Rehaan and whispered, 'Perfect; just perfect.' Sumer took the cue and excused himself on the pretext of getting us drinks. 'Mom won't come...but just in case, she does, he is Resham...my school friend,' he said and closed the door. We went and sat on one bean bag together. A few seconds later, my phone beeped. I read Sumer's message:

'Just be quick...Siddhartha is on his way.
Don't be naughty, naughty.

P.S. AIDS se bacchein.

'Asshole,' I said and smiled as Rehaan snuggled upto me. We were together in a room after a long time.

'What?' he asked.

'Nothing, baby,' I said and turned around. Thanks to my best friend that my boyfriend and I shared a long passionate kiss.

15

Bed and Good-Time Buddies

September

When he...well, no comments.

'Why doesn't Mom understand? Why the hell does she not understand? Ugh, why? Why?' I asked the question superficially like a stale news channel does in different painfully haunting modulations.

'So, which part of the last three sentences qualifies to be counted in the "urgent, please call" message you sent me two minutes ago?' Sumer asked and yawned to signify that he had been disturbed out of his sleep.

'You...you sleepster,' I shouted into the phone. It was just 1.30 a.m. and this guy wanted to sleep, when his best friend was about to weep. 'Sumer, you are a beep, beep and another beep.'

'Whatever, I am tired,' he said and cut the phone.

My anger rose as quickly as the male tool does in response to a verbal and visual stimuli. I pressed '4' on the keypad of my cell and the speed dial did the rest.

'Hello.'

'You son of a bi...beautiful aunty! How dare you slam the

phone on me?' I shouted, trying to vent my unfamiliar and familiar frustration.

'I didn't cut it; my balance finished,' he shouted back. Louder shouts silence the not-so-loud shouts. I took a deep breath.

'But I got your phone recharged for a 100 bucks today morning,' I said surprised. Imagine the world believes that only women talk!

'Excuse me, but I have a girlfriend who lives in another state.

'So, can't she call?' I questioned.

'She exhausted her top up first yaar.' For how long had they been talking, I wondered!

'We talked for some three hours and two minutes, you see,' he automatically transformed the assumption into a fact.

'Sumer, it's people like you who render the phenomenon of ear cancer all the more familiar,' I sarcastically added.

He ignored it. 'So what doesn't aunty understand?'

'That meeting or talking with a boy won't turn me into a slut,' I repeated the statement for the third time. My other two best friends could explain further.

'It's okay yaar, and you are talking with me. I mean I am a boy,' he seemed to assure himself rather than me. I smiled.

'But you are hardly a boy...you sleep all the time. I bet you are sleepy right now as well,' I said devilishly.

'I was just tired yaar...anyway, what happened exactly?' he clarified and then questioned.

I wanted a clearer view on his clarification. 'What made you so tired?'

'It's been a long day, *tan-tan*,' he said and yawned wide enough to diffuse a full bottle of carbon dioxide in the room.

'Oh yeah! What have you done for the whole day except to get up, eat breakfast, go to school, again eat during recess, come back and eat lunch at home, sleep, missing the Maths tuition, then get up in the evening and eat out with your friends. That's the end.'

'Okay, I get it,' he stopped me from completing his tiring day's schedule which on economic parameters pointed to a definitely depressed economy or a waste of human resource.

'I was tired because I was talking to Liaka,' he offered. Did I just mention the words 'guilty conscience' somewhere?

'So, talking to Liaka makes you tired? If this was a Facebook status, she would have disliked you and then reported abuse against you. I joked.

'Well, it can get me worked up sometimes,' he said in a funny tone.

'Oh my God! Were you working out? I mean, doing ding-dong on the phone?' I got up in my bed.

'So, you still didn't tell me about what exactly happened with aunty?' he asked, clearly displaying his intention to avoid answering.

'With her? Nothing, but...you tell me, what were you up to, Dhillon?' I demanded.

'Okay Tanie, yes, I was kind of ding-donging,' he said confidently. I bet he must have got up in his bed too.

'Oye hoye! Hey, but wait a second, it took you three hours to...?' I left the sentence open to interpretation.

'Actually no, yaar. The first time the volcano was on the verge of eruption. Her top up ended and the lava cooled down quickly,' he said devoid of any apprehension. We laughed. What else could one expect from *besharam* best friends?

'And then?' I asked.

'Then I called her up and by the time the white waterfall mode could begin, her Mom came into the room and she cut the phone.' We laughed again.

'So you didn't call her back?' I asked the dumbest question.

'Obviously, Tanie, duh...but her phone was switched off after that,' he replied.

'The "mother problem" is universal I think,' I concluded.

'So, what is aunty exactly unable to understand?' he asked politely for an impolite moment.

'That life without boys is like umm...a KFC without the chicken...' We both laughed.

'So, seriously what happened in between?' I stopped the question midway.

'Mom's friend saw me with Rehaan at the lake,' I said casually. Seven hours back, on the live scene, I was almost in tears.

'And then?' he asked. It took me fifteen minutes to explain him the details and laugh in between. 'So you told your Mom you met him by chance?' he asked again.

'No yaar, I said I bumped into him while jogging.'

'Wait a second, since when did you start going for a jog at the lake, Tanie?'

'This was the same question that Mom asked me,' I replied and we both started laughing again. 'I mean she has to understand yaar that I am not a lesbian.'

'So, according to you, girls who don't have a boyfriend are?' he asked.

'Huh! Even Megha said, I mean, asked the same question some time back.'

We laughed again. 'So is aunty really pissed off?' he inquired next.

'I don't think so yaar. She would have taken my cell phone otherwise.'

'Oh, I see,' he, for some strange reason, whispered.

'Oi, I just realized that you said both of you reached the climax but the curtains fell before time, right?' I asked, interested again.

'Hmmm...that's a nice way to phrase it,' he commented and we laughed.

'So don't you feel like doing it now?' I asked him.

'You have a nice, useful, imaginative and supportive feminine voice Tanie Brar,' he whispered again, hoarsely.

'Oh God, you are sick, Sumer!'

'Yes baby...Yes, yes, yes...,' and then suddenly he fell silent.

'Sumer...Sumer...,' I whispered.

Suddenly he began, 'Ya...a...aah...ah...a...ha, just kidding yaar.'

I cleared my throat in relief, 'You scared me for a moment there.'

'Scared, why?' he asked normally.

'Well, having it on the phone with your best friend is umm... scary,' I concluded.

'*Na*, not really,' he said.

'It is,' I said.

'Trust me, it isn't.' The coolness in his voice had started to give me goosebumps all over again.

'Oh yeah, how can you...?' Before I could continue, a low moan interrupted me. 'Fuckkk,' I whispered aloud.

'What?' he asked surprised.

'JERK, I know you were jerking,' I had to say it out.

'Huh, you are fantasizing...I wasn't jerking. I just sneezed,' he said.

'You moaned,' I accused.

'It is a low-decibel sneeze,' he said in explanation.

'Whatever,' I said and cut the call. Till today, I wonder if it was a sneeze or....ugh!

16

Boards, Buddies and Break ups

1 December

I flipped the table calendar kept on Sumer's table to December. 'Do you ever use it?'

He was lying down on his bed with his Hindi *MPH Guide* in hand pre-Board exams were close enough to let us feel sulky, depressed and down (well, in my case only!).

'Twenty-four hours, one thousand four hundred forty minutes...a day begins, a night ends and then after thirty such cycles, the month ends...' Such cynical stuff coming from Sumer never meant good news.

I walked up to his bed and sat on the edge, the calendar in hand. 'Did you and Liaka fight again?' I asked calmly. Ten minutes of my stipulated one hour evening break from books had already been wasted and how!

He got up, sat in his bed, closed his book and without answering me, opened his laptop. I took a deep breath.

'Hey, look at this—after Monday, Tuesday, even the calendar is like w...t...f.' My joke had the desired effect—a familiar arc graced his lips. He looked up from the laptop screen.

'Tanie, you are a girl, right?'

'Ummm...yes,' I replied.

'Tell me from a girl's point of view, am I insensitive?' he asked emotionally. Was there irony somewhere?

'No...I mean, yeah, you can be a jerk, a pervert, an idiot and a moron but the best part is that you're caring,' I smiled convincingly.

'Why the fuck can't Liaka see it then? I mean, c'mon I call her every day, chat on the webcam with her every night, send her gifts through e-bay, even complete her English homework. What else does she want? I also have to study. My Dad, you know, he will be here soon and he'll screw me with I don't know what, if I don't score in these pre-Boards,' he said in one go.

I remained silent.

'What?' he demanded, closing the laptop screen, in his sulky tone. 'We have been together for two years now and still sometimes I feel we hardly know each other...and look at you, not even a year and you know me so well.'

'Sorry Dhillon, if this is one of your sad attempts at hitting on me...I'm already taken, buddy,' I joked and threw a pillow at him playfully. He caught hold of it and hugged it.

'That's the whole problem,' he stressed.

'What?' I asked.

'That you are taken...it would have been so much more easier, so convenient...just like now. You're here in my room, on my bed, so close to me,' he said seductively.

'Dog,' I got up immediately. 'No more meeting you behind closed doors,' I said sternly and we both laughed. 'And Mr Sumer, did I just hear that you both video chat every night?' It was my turn to talk trash.

A blush crept on his face immediately, 'Well, let's just say, Liaka still likes to see my tattoo. Do you want to see it again?'

he asked playing with his T-shirt.

'Hell, no! I still can't believe how my Mom thinks you're an angel.'

He laughed heartily and got up from his bed. 'Do you want to go for a walk?' he asked me.

We both could seriously do with some fresh air. 'Okay, but only on one condition,' I stressed.

'What?'

'Liaka...will accompany us.'

'Yes...Liaka, the bitch.'

He laughed, I laughed, problem solved.

10 December

'Hey,' Sumer greeted impatiently.

'Hi Sumer! How is your preparation coming along?' Megha, who had called from my cell, asked him in her sweeter-than-Cadbury voice.

'Oh Megha, hi! So?'

'So nothing, Sumer. Can't I even call you, *haan*? It seems that you have forgotten me...no calls, no messages, not even a "hi". Are you angry with me?' Damsels and dramatics go hand in hand. I giggled from behind as Megha put the phone on loudspeaker.

'It's just that Dad's back and these pre-Boards...You have Maths tomorrow, right?'

'Yes, sigh! Tanie and I are revising together.'

'Where's Tanie?' he asked. Finally!

'So I do exist...lucky me,' I said with a superficial hurt.

'No yaar! Tanie it's not like that,' he said, trying to hide his shortcoming.

'Chill, Sumer. Anyway, all set for Science tomorrow?' I asked him.

'Yeah, I think, I'm glad reproduction carries eight marks in Biology,' he said and laughed. Megha and I exchanged a 'how typical' look.

'And you know, what happened today?' he suddenly exclaimed.

'What?' we asked together.

'I was practising the Biology diagrams and Dad walked up to me just when I was drawing the female, you know.'

'Yeah, we understand,' Megha said quickly. His voice on loudspeaker was booming enough in her huge room.

'Yeah, so Dad walked up to me and he goes like...' He imitated his Dad's voice, 'Well, this looks totally different in reality.' We all burst out laughing.

'I wish my parents were so cool...my Mom almost fainted when she saw the male organ image in my book,' Megha mumbled and we laughed some more.

'So Sumer...actually I had called you for a reason.' I finally announced the purpose of the call after fifteen minutes of well-kind-of-dirty talk. 'Rehaan and I complete a year on this 22nd' and I remember him once talking about this blue coloured Ed Hardy T-shirt that you have.'

'You want to gift him my T-shirt? How cheap can you get Tanie?'

'Ugh! I want you to order the same T-shirt from eBay. I have e-mailed you the link and yes, I will pay for it,' I said sincerely, even though I knew Sumer would never accept a penny from me.

'Oh? Okay, I'll order it and about the money...'

I shot Megha the sly work-done-for-free smile. Have a rich, courteous best friend; it helps.

'If you could pay in cash by tomorrow, I'd appreciate,' he said and the phone cut, leaving behind two shocked girls on the other line.

We went back to studying till my cell phone beeped again. It was Sumer.

'If you both have overcome the shock, open your e-mail and check out the shoes I have ordered alongside...a gift from me for my best friend's boyfriend.'

I smiled and asked Megha to get her laptop.

After checking the shoes and T-shirt, I replied, continuing with the senti stuff.

'Thank you, but I...seriously want to pay.'

He replied in no time.

'Anything for your happiness, Tanie...'

P.S. You can pay me in other ways too...think about it. Now study and let me study as well.'

I laughed here, he laughed there, problem solved.

13 December
Seven hours before the Social Science pre-Board
Airtel *zindabad*!

Sumer: 'Hey, did I disturb you?'

Tanie: 'I feel suicidal...History is so...'

Sumer (faintly laughing): 'Join the club.'

Sumer: 'How's Rehaan?'

Tanie: 'Good, was just talking with him. His accounts pre-Board is tomorrow.'

Sumer (low voice): 'You both are so lucky to have each other.'

Tanie: 'What's wrong?'

Sumer: 'Nothing; just like that.'

Tanie: 'You can't even lie properly.'

Sumer (faint laugh): 'We fought again.'

Tanie: 'Again!'

Sumer: 'It was her fault.'

Tanie: 'Long-distance relationships...well, what happened exactly?'

Sumer: 'I myself don't know...things are changing.'

Tanie: 'And you're letting them change?'

Sumer: 'This is our fifth argument this month...I don't know how she is managing her pre-Boards like this? (Silence) Tanie, say something, will you?'

Tanie: 'You know what, Sumer? I think you are at fault too.'

Sumer: 'Why do you say that?'

Tanie: 'Cause you remember the number of times you've fought...not the times you've spent laughing or living for each other. (Silence) Sumer, are you there?'

Sumer (muffled voice): 'All the best for tomorrow... Bye'

Tanie: 'Sumer..., no wait.'

The call got disconnected and I tried calling again. 'The Airtel number you are trying to reach is currently switched off,' came the voice.

20 December

Dreaded dark circles, carelessly chipped nails, dangerously dull faces, unthreaded eyebrows, obnoxious oily hair—the after-effects of giving pre-Boards, the prelude to the big B and to rightly detoxify the study germs—Stuti, Megha and I directly visited Megha's salon after our last exam had ended.

We needed the pump, especially me, as 22nd was just a day away. My baby and I were completing a year together and I had every right to jump deep into the sea of cleansing creams, hot hair spa and fresh wax.

'Aah, this is heaven!' Megha exclaimed. We three were sitting in one of the cubicles, our feet dipped in pedicure tubs. I tried calling Rehaan again...I had been doing the same, ever since I had come out of the examination hall.

'Not picking up your phone?' Megha asked, eyeing my upset eyes.

'No...must be busy somewhere.' I didn't know why but a sinking feeling was mixing in my blood.

'Yeah, so what are you gifting him? It's a big, big day, after all,' asked Stuti to brighten things up. Megha tried to add humour, 'C'mon Stuti, I told you the other day...you always seem to forget. Obviously Tanie will gift her vir...'

'Shut up Megha, it's not funny,' I snapped at the other two giggling girls.

'What? I was just telling her about the stuff Sumer got delivered for Rehaan,' she said, trying hard to get that innocent look into her eyes.

My cell rang and I almost jumped in excitement. I picked it up.

'Sumer...oh, hi,' I greeted him in a low tone.

'Hey, Tanie, where are you?' his generally jovial voice held urgency. 'Is everything alright?'

Megha and Stuti shot me a quizzing look.

'Yeah...everything is fine. Listen, when will you reach back home?'

'In the evening. Are you sure that everything is alright?'

I got up, wore my shoes and walked out of the cubicle. 'Hang on for a second,' I said and continued walking towards the main door of the salon.

'Yeah, did you and Liaka fight again?' I asked as soon as I reached outside.

'No, we didn't fight or anything...actually I was out with Uday and the other guys from school. We were celebrating the post pre-Boards freedom. And while we were on our way to PVR cinemas, Uday got a call from his mother. She needed some medicines and we were in his car. So, we went to his sector's market and at the chemist Uday saw Rehaan.' He paused momentarily, as if carefully choosing his words. 'This might be normal also...just don't overreact or anything.'

'What was Rehaan doing over there?' I interjected immediately.

'Tanie, listen, where are you right now?' he asked calmly.

'At Megha's salon,' I replied in an exactly opposite tone.

'Okay...where is it?' his patience was making me impatient.

'Sumer, can you just tell me what was Rehaan doing over there. Please,' I pleaded.

'Okay listen, don't cry or anything. You know I hate it when you cry. Everybody is inside in the theatre...I'll ask Uday's driver to drop me at Megha's salon. Ten minutes exactly.'

'Sumer, do you realize that I just got a facial thirty minutes ago and this tension is doing no good to my face?' I tried to joke. Humour was the only thing that could coax him to come out with what he was hiding.

'Ten minutes...from now,' he said and cut the line.

I called him again.

'Ten minutes Tanie...I said ten,' he pleaded this time.

'Idiot...you didn't even take the address,' I said and forced out a little laugh and believe me, it took a mammoth effort.

Some eight minutes later

Stuti and Megha were randomly guessing about the various possibilities when the cell phone rang again. I picked it up on the second ring.'

'I'm outside the salon...should I walk in?' he asked and I repeated the same question to Megha. Her parents might be the richest but definitely weren't the coolest ones around.

I wore my shoes, tucked in my school shirt, adjusted my skirt and walked outside. Sumer's uniform was a shade better than mine, in terms of appearance.

'Hi,' he extended his hand, like for the first time in a chivalrous way.

'Hi,' I held it.

'Your hair...looks nice.' Yes, Sumer complimented me out of the blue.

'Thank you.'

'Nice day, isn't it?'

'Shut up, Dhillon, you know you can't act to save your life,' I snapped and despite the tension, both of us started laughing.

We both decided to go to Barista, four shops ahead.

'So?' I inhaled deeply after we were seated in Barista. Sumer was just about to speak as the waiter came and interrupted him.

'Sir,' he gave Sumer the menu and shot him a schoolchildren-bunking-and-doing-haw-stuff look.

'Sumer *bhaiya*,' I touched his hand to dispel all the useless thoughts the waiter was dwelling on and continued, 'I'll have a capuccino.'

'Make it two capuccinos, one brownie, one chicken sandwich...I think that's all for now,' he said. How could I forget that food preceded friends for this monster of a best friend. The waiter took the order and left.

'Okay...now that you have ordered enough for a light year, can you please tell me what happened?' I asked, my intuition working against what my heart wanted to believe.

'Tanie, have you and Rehaan...I mean don't get me wrong here but have you both been like...,' he stopped again.

'What, Sumer?' I gasped.

'I just don't know how to say this.'

'Sumer, stop irritating me. It's not like you have never said something weird or cheap before.'

'Okay fine. Has Rehaan been screwing you?'

My hand shot up in reflex and he dodged it. The couple

sitting on the next table shot me a sympathetic look, like Sumer was dumping me or something.

'I have told you before as well...this is one thing I will never do. I just won't...I am not so cheap!' I said loudly and the girl in the couple almost got up from her seat. Was she coming to console me?

'Don't shout, okay? Have some water,' Sumer offered the the glass and I reluctantly drained half of it.

'Tanie, listen. I didn't mean to upset you or anything. It's just that Uday saw Rehaan buying condoms from the chemist... and he told me and I thought I should tell you. I have told him to shut up about the whole thing though.'

Silence! That's what spoke for the next two painfully long minutes and then my voice killed it. 'He must be mistaken... it's impossible,' was all I had to say.

'I'd also thought so, but then Uday called me from the chemist and I got down from the car and walked up to him... but by that time Rehaan had left. So we followed the path Uday had seen him take and then I saw him buying cigarettes from the roadside vendor.'

'Impossible. Rehaan doesn't smoke. I...I...' I lowered my voice to a hiss, 'I have kissed him; he doesn't smoke.'

'Even that's what I thought, Tanie. That you obviously would know,' he stopped, embarrassed as the waiter arrived with the order. We stayed silent till he left. 'But the fact is that I did see him light a cigarette,' he stressed.

'You must have seen someone else, yaar.'

He opened his mouth to speak and then kept quiet, only to question me after a few seconds, 'Will do you me a favour?'

'What?'

'Will you prove me wrong?'

'I'd love to.'

'Okay, call him and ask him what was he doing at the chemist at 12.30 p.m. in Sector 6? Ask him if he is alright? I mean, act concerned and stuff.' I had never seen someone plan his own downfall before.

'Okay, but I am doing this not because I don't trust him or anything but because I want to prove you wrong,' I said and dialled his number and turned the cell phone to loudspeaker, while Sumer sat there silent and still, not even touching the brownie. Rehaan didn't pick up the call again.

'He hasn't been taking my calls since morning,' I regretted, opening my mouth as soon as I finished the sentence. Sumer's hopeless belief was getting hope after all.

Rehaan finally picked up the seventh call made to him. Before I could say anything he began, 'If I am not picking your call it obviously means I am busy,' he said angrily. I felt my cheeks burn. Sumer also heard him shout.

'I'm sorry,' I said in a low voice and his tone changed.

'You don't have to apologize, Tanie. I've been studying since today morning. Unlike you, I still have an exam tomorrow, baby.'

Sumer started waving his hands frantically, signalling me to speed up the conversation.

'Uh...Rehaan, were you by any chance at the chemist in Sector 6 at 12.30 p.m.?' I asked him carefully.

Rehaan took some time to reply, 'Me? No, I haven't stepped out of the house since morning,' he paused. 'Why?'

'Nothing, Sumer must have seen someone else then.'

'Rehaan...come here,' a female voice interjected from behind.

'Who is that?' I asked impulsively.

'Mm...Mom. Listen, I'll call you in the evening. Okay? Muwah.' He cut the line in the next second.

Sumer was intently looking into my eyes.

'What, he's studying for the exam tomorrow,' I didn't know why I stammered.

His grave expression still did not change.

'What, Sumer?' I laughed uneasily.

He reached for my hand and squeezed it in his warm palm. 'Do you believe me?' he asked softly.

'Sumer, see, I did whatever you told me to. You're mistaken.' Then why was I feeling guilty and unsure myself?

'Do you believe me or not?' he asked, still holding my hand. I closed my eyes and Rehaan's face flashed before my eyes—no, how could I go weak and not trust him? I loved him; he was the reason why I breathed.

'Sumer…,' my lament had no effect.

He sighed.

'What Dhillon?' I tried to act normal.

'Nothing…I…I think I'll leave now,' he signalled the waiter for the cheque.

'Sumer, c'mon. Okay, don't stay for me but what about all this food?' I knew he wouldn't say no to it…

'I've had more than I can digest,' he said and got up and walked straight to the washroom.

'Are you done?' he asked me after he came back, two minutes later. His eyes seemed different…they seemed distant. He walked me back to the salon. 'Bye,' he said and turned around and walked to the car—a little teary-eyed.

An hour later, outside PVR cinemas

'Tanie is calling again,' Uday, who was holding Sumer's cell, stated.

'Let her,' Sumer replied with extra casualness.

'Okay,' Uday reluctantly said, giving the phone back to Sumer.

24

10 minutes later; in the car

The missed calls had tolled up to eight now.

'I bought this new console for my PC. You want to check it out?' Uday asked, as Sumer continued to stare out of the window silently.

'Just drop me home, man,' he muttered.

'Oh c'mon, if Tanie doesn't care, why do you?' Uday said.

'Because I care for her dammit...that guy...he is bloody using her, he is a &&*C (*#*@(#*#(#*,' Sumer's pent up frustration finally found the vocal channel.

'Okay, let me plug in some metal...you can shout out your balls then,' Uday said supportively as his cell phone started ringing. 'Tanie is calling me now...Should I pick it up?' he asked carefully.

'Do whatever you want,' Sumer's voice was nothing more than an angry whisper.

Uday picked up my dying call.

'Hello!'

'Hi Uday,' I said cheerfully, feeling within like shit. 'Ummm... is Sumer with you?' I asked.

'Hey Tanie, can you hold on for a second? I'm getting another call,' Uday quickly put me on hold and repeated my question to Sumer.

'Tell her I am with you. But I don't want to talk with her,' Sumer said and Uday repeated the same for me.

I sighed; irritation had seen birth. 'Can you put the cell phone on loudspeaker, Uday?' Megha and Stuti sat listening with escalating curiosity. Uday followed the instructions and I began, 'Sumer?'

No reply. The patience in my voice was giving way.

'Sumer, please...'

No reply.

My patience murdered,
the kindness expunged.

'Listen Sumer, I am not fucking mad that I have been calling you like a fucking...a fucking...a fucking...'

'Chocolate,' Megha added from behind and I repeated without thinking what I was saying. 'Sorry,' Megha held her ears as I shot her a dirty look.

'Yes, Sumer, if you don't want to talk to me, fine. I have full faith in my boyfriend, but you know what the problem is?' No reply but I continued anyway. 'Unlike you, I trust the person I love.'

Megha touched my shoulder in order to make me stop but the anger drive in me had no intention to press the brakes. 'And you really won't understand because even after two years, you and Liaka are heading nowhere,' I breathed heavily.

No reply—the venomous silence stung.

'Oh, I got it now. You wanted to create a rift between me and Rehaan. It's actually my fault...Rehaan was right about you from day one.'

Anger does it—illuminating the dark secrets, giving voice to unsaid words. He was still silent.

'Now say something, will you?' I barked loudly and the call ended. Uday had cut the call on noticing Sumer's clouded eyes.

❦

Some dark, dreaded hours later.

Mom knocked at my door.

'What?' I shouted angrily. I had locked myself in my room

as soon as I reached back home.

Do you mind opening the door?'

'Yes I do.'

'Sumer is here,' she said uneasily.

I began to say something and then stopped. I got up from my bed, picked up a compass kept on my study table and walked towards the door, debating if I should let my mother witness her daughter stab someone without any mercy. I stopped at the door as my mind struck with another perverted idea, 'Mom, tell Sumer to F.O.'

'F.O.?' Then I heard Mom ask Sumer what it meant. Revenge...Ahh! Putting your best friend in an embarrassing situation with your mother—how nice!

'Aunty, it's umm...ummm...flush off,' I heard him explain and to enjoy his agonized expression, I quickly opened the door. Contrary to expectations, I found Mom and him smiling.

'What?' I demanded with folded hands.

'Nothing sweetie, it's just that parents aren't as näive as you think them to be,' she said and left to ask the servant to prepare cold coffee for us.

I briefly glanced at Sumer. He was carrying a bag. 'Must be a sorry card or an apology gift inside,' I thought and felt the cold compass burn in the warmth of my hand.

I walked back inside my room and went to my study table to keep the compass back. He walked in behind me and cleared his throat to apologize.

'I haven't come here to apologize,' were the first words he said.

'Uhh...okay,' I swallowed down the shock.

'I just came to give this,' he slung the bag off his shoulder and unzipped it to take out a polythene bag which had eBay written on it in bold letters. He handed the polythene bag to me and slurred, 'You don't have to pay me or anything...my friendship is not so cheap.'

With the packet in my hand, I had only two choices—the gift versus my self-esteem or the satisfaction of throwing the packet on Sumer's face versus the satisfaction of the smile that on seeing the gift would grace Rehaan's face; about me versus about we; about my self-respect or Rehaan's happiness. The latter won hands down. I let myself fail for Rehaan to rise... but then, this is what love is!

'I have seen how cheap you can be,' I said coldly to Sumer, not even showing the slightest attempt to return him the packet.

'You'll realize...one day you will realize and you know what, I'll still be there for you...because I always considered you my closest friend,' he said emotionally, turned around and walked out of my life.

22 December

'There, that's his car!' Megha said excitedly as a black Skoda pulled up in front of the foyer of the mall. I shivered. This was it...everything had been turned out to be surprisingly so smooth. Mom hadn't objected to my supposed movie-and-lunch plan with my girlfriends. We three had reached my pickup point well before time—Megha's Gucci skirt and stockings and my Mango sweater draped me in beauty; my hair had the shine, lips the gloss, eyes the sparkle, nails the shimmer and heart the love.

I quickly took the gift from Stuti's hand and started the rapid fire round again with my best friends.

'Do I look fine?'

'Yes.'

'Do I smell good?' 'Yes!'

'Oh and...stockings—is the length fine?'

'Yes Tanie...chill!'

'And...my breath...haaa, how does it smell?'

'You have had so much of mint...it's obviously fresh.'

'Oh shit, I am feeling scared.'

'Go Tanie, he is waiting...we will meet you here after three hours. Enjoy your day.'

'Yeah, enjoy the movie.'

'Bye!'

'Bye!' I started walking towards the car. Every step was marked by an unknown sensation. If Sumer had seen me now, he would have understood how much Rehaan and I loved each other, but only if Sumer and I had been talking now. I cleared my mind of all thoughts and opened the door of Rehaan's car.

He was seated inside—dressed in a white sweater and blue denims...totally edible! He extended his hungry arm, asking for my hand. I extended it and he literally pulled me inside. I crashed softly on the passenger seat and he, taking advantage of the 60 per cent black-tinted glasses, kissed me passionately for a second.

'I love you,' I gasped.

'Happy anniversary, baby,' he fished out a small box from his pocket and placed it on my hand. I gave him my gift and urged him to open it.

'Let's get out of here first,' he kept my gift on the back seat and started to drive.

I didn't know where we were heading to and with him by my side, I seriously saw no reason to ask. The day was surprisingly sunny; the car and my heart romantically warm; his face charming; the music soft...bliss abounded. Everything was just perfect!

His cell phone, which was kept on the gear box, started to ring. Out of natural curiosity and the fact that he was driving, I reached for it.

'Who is it?' he asked.

'It says...Mom calling.' I was about to pick up the call when he snatched the phone away from my hand. Everyone in Rehaan's family knew about us. I had even met aunty and his sister many times. So, why did he snatch the cell?

'She doesn't know I'm with you,' he explained after he saw the confusion on my face and then started to talk, 'Yes?' he said strangely.

A shrilly feminine, not-so-motherly voice boomed out of the cell phone.

'Slowly...don't shout...I am with someone,' he juggled between stealing looks at me, driving and the call.

'Who are you with?' the feminine voice demanded. Somehow, despite the sunshine, I started to feel cold. I waited for him to reply with bated breath.

'I am with a friend,' said he and the apprehension in me knew no bounds. Sumer's words haunted me again.

'Okay, bye! Yes, I'll get your phone's top up as soon as possible,' I heard Rehaan shout and then he cut the phone, keeping it back on the gear box. It wasn't summer...yet he brushed his hand against his forehead and wiped off the glistening liquid drops.

'Is everything alright?' I didn't know why I stammered.

'Uh...yes. It was my sister. I had to get her cell recharged... so she called me from Mom's cell and blasted me off,' he replied sweetly.

'Then why did you lie to her about me?' I asked in a low voice.

He laughed loudly, 'Because princess, she would have then asked me to make her meet you and I don't want to share you with anybody. Not today, at least.'

A confident smile broke on my face. I cursed my imagination

for running wild and took his hand from the gear in mine. I kissed his hand and felt it against my cheeks.

'Don't Tanie, it'll be difficult for me to drive,' he joked and freed his hand.

'Where are we going?' I asked him next. He just smiled. 'Tell me baby,' I urged him.

'Okay, right now, we are going to the nearest mobile shop and getting my sister's cell recharged.'

We found a mobile shop after two minutes. He stopped his car on the opposite side of the road.

'I'll be back in two minutes. You want something?' he asked and opened the door.

'Yes...a big Dairy Milk,' I said cutely and he smiled and got out, leaving the car in ignition and his cell phone behind.

Sitting alone with nothing else to do, I started to search for a particular CD, which had my favourite song. I flipped through the CD case, looked in the door pockets but couldn't find it. 'The dashboard', I thought and opened it, rumbling through the car papers, manual, first-aid kit, deo bottles and what not trash it concealed. Just as I was about to close the dashboard, I chanced to look upon a match-box kept inside.

A boulder dropped in a pond somewhere and the splash reached my eyes. Before I could conclude anything, his cell phone started ringing and I picked it up to see 'Mom' flashing on it again. Call it my insecurity or my subconscious desire to prove Sumer wrong, I picked up the call. Before I could say 'Hello', I heard a female shout again, 'Listen Rehaan, I know you are with that little kiddo...and you don't want me to call you again and again, but don't forget that it is me who you come to at the end of the day. It is me who you have been screwing for the past six months. So you better get my phone recharged in the next two minutes or you know what I'm capable of. 9***—isn't this that little dumb, innocent ATM's number? Poor girl! She thinks you love her...Haa!' The cell phone slipped from my hand and as I bent down to retrieve it, I tasted salt. I didn't know what exactly overtook me then—a rage for revenge or the pain of getting shattered or just true love while being hurt. I wiped my tears and pulled down the window. I could see Rehaan's distant figure; even the few metres that separated us now, felt like milestones. A fresh round of tears invaded my eyes and I blinked hard to expunge them.

What happened next? I still don't know what thought process initiated it—I took out the key from the ignition and picked up his cell phone. Then I turned around and got hold of the unopened gift before jumping out of the car. I saw Rehaan starting to walk towards me...the busy two-way traffic not allowing him to cross the road. Whatever possessed me, I still don't know. I picked up a big stone from the road and with all my might, I fiercely scratched something on his car.

'Tanie...what are you doing?' I heard Rehaan shout from the opposite end. One look at him and the passion and intensity of my hands knew no bounds. I could feel the rough stone's edges cut me, but they were nothing in comparison to the wound Rehaan had inflicted on my heart. I threw the stone after five seconds and started to run towards a stationary radio taxi parked at a distance. The next minute I was in the taxi, going far away from Rehaan and a Skoda on which a new message had been etched, 'Don't screw your "Mom" again!'

Five minutes later

'Hello! Sumer?' I fought back the tears and squeaked.

'Tanie...what's wrong?' he asked immediately.

'Sumer...,' I choked. 'Sumer you were right...you were right about everything.' Tears hindered my vision. The old taxi-driver asked me if everything was alright. I wiped my tears and murmured a feeble 'yes'.

'Where are you?' asked Sumer.

'In the taxi...Sumer, how could he?'

'Come to my house...no one is here.'

'But Mom...she doesn't know,' I began.

'Your Mom and my Mom have gone shopping...just come now and please stop crying because I can't bear it.'

I instructed the clueless taxi-driver on the destination.

'Are you still there?' I asked weakly.

'Yes Tanie...I am,' he paused, 'always for you.'

'How could he Sumer...I loved him.'

'Don't cry Tanie.... and keep quiet now.'

'But...'

'Shhh...'

'I love.'

'Shhh...just be quiet.'

'Mmm...'

'Quiet Tanie, just close your eyes and rest, till you reach here...I'm standing at the gate.'

૨૪

'It's okay...easy,' Sumer helped me out of the taxi and paid the taxi driver. 'Come, let's go inside before Mrs Anjali gets to see me hug you,' he joked and I smiled into his shirt. Just as we were walking towards the main door, the taxi-driver called out to us. Sumer asked me to go inside while he went back to the driver.

I was sitting on the stairs inside, when he returned.

'Who's mobile is this and whose keys are these?' he asked and before I could answer, the mobile started ringing. Sumer looked at me sitting mutely and picked up the call.

'Hello,' he said apprehensively.

'Hello...who is this? Where is Tanie?' Rehaan's angry voice reached me even though Sumer was standing at the door.

'Its Sumer...' he said calmly.

'Where is Tanie?' he demanded.

'She is with me Rehaan...don't call her again,' Sumer said maturely.

'I won't have the bitch take my cell phone and my car keys.' Sumer looked at my overflowing eyes.

'What?' he asked softly.

'Can't you hear? That little bitch took my keys and my cell phone...I will kill her.' His loud shouts shattered me completely and I started howling, only to stop after hearing Sumer swear at Rehaan continuously for I don't know how long. All I heard was, 'So you better understand...get anyone you want, any fucking guy with you...if you want to fight...c'mon I don't give...but I won't stand another abuse for Tanie.'

The rage in Sumer's eyes scared me. He continued, 'Your keys and cell phone are kept outside in my letter-box. Take them from here and yes, if you still have the balls, ring my bell and you will see what I do to you.' Sumer marched outside and closed the main door loudly.

I sat there transfixed till he returned. He was on a call with somebody, 'Yes...Rehaan, Standard VII. He is coming to my house...yeah, okay...' he smiled. 'I know, I'm scared for him; not for myself. Right! Thank you,' he disconnected and went to the kitchen to return with a water bottle.

'You don't have to worry about anything, Tanie. This guy I was talking to, I had met him at the local swimming pool. He knows Rehaan...in fact, he just called him a ***t,' he smiled and sat down next to me.

'S....s....Sumer,' I stammered.

'Shhhh...' His warm embrace was what I needed and got. 'You don't have to worry...he won't trouble you again.'

'Sumer...,' I stammered again.

'Tanie...stop crying. I told you he won't trouble you again... trust me this time,' he weakly joked.

'I never knew you could be so macho,' I said and then we both started smiling...then softly laughing...then laughing beyond control...only for me to end up crying softly into his shirt. He kept on caressing my hair, asking me to keep quiet while I tried my best to obey. Then, I don't know when it began or why it happened, but it just did—Sumer was kissing me and I was kissing him back.

A *few seconds later*

'I love you,' Sumer whispered in my ear and I suddenly opened my eyes and broke the embrace. 'What happened?' he asked softly.

'No Sumer,' I whined.

'What Tanie?' he reached out for my hand but I rejected his attempts.

'I loved Rehaan...I still love Rehaan and this...this kiss...I feel like a slut...'

'Don't say that Tanie...please don't. Liaka and I are virtually not together any more and you know how much we care for each other,' his voice had an appeal.

'No Sumer, I can't love you. My love for him was genuine...I can't be like him; I can't love you.' I got up from the stairs in haste and walked towards the main door.

'Tanie...please.' The same guy who had been shouting some minutes ago was pleading now.

'Bye, Sumer,' I said and walked out. That was the last time Sumer and I ever talked to each other.

17

Love and Friendship Go Hand in Hand

Aaryan
THE PRESENT

'Here,' I said, handing Tanie the leftover, unused tissue papers from our lunch tray. Two little drops of salt had hijacked her eyes and my heart.

'I immersed myself in studies—just books and me; no friends, no movies, no Sumer…He tried to talk to me so many times after that but I never reciprocated, so finally he gave up too. January and February passed somehow to give way to March and the Boards. Just when the cobwebs of convenience were about to settle in, Sumer came back again in my life. The night before I was to come here, he came to my house and gave me a note. He had asked me one simple question.

'So do you have your answer now?' I asked her.

'I don't know. Rehaan…what about him? Moving on makes me feel like a…,' she continued in a very low voice to add 'slut.'

'What about Ishita? I had wondered too,' I told her.

'Yes…Ishita. What happened with her? You met her, right?' I smiled, 'No.'

'No? But why not? You both had started talking too. Then why? Did she not want to meet you?'

'She wanted to meet me but I didn't meet her,' I replied.

'Why?' a superlative surprise is what her frame radiated.

'We shall be landing shortly. Please return to your seats and fasten your seatbelts,' the speakers came to life, before I could answer her.

'I should return,' I said and got up.

She started to say something but then pursed her lips, her expression resigned, her eyes screaming, 'No!. 'Okay,' she said.

I smiled and started to move, 'Oh, I forgot. This is for you, Tanie. It rightly belongs to you now.' I kept the book I was carrying on the seat I had occupied previously and started to move. She turned around and kept staring as I started to walk back to my seat. I stopped after some steps and said loudly, 'Don't look so incomplete...you already have an answer...You just need to read it.'

'Read what?' her voice came across as a shout. Everybody was looking at us along with the airhostess, who was giving me a go-and-strap-your-seatbelt, you-asshole look.

'The book...it's *A Walk to Remember*,' I said, turned and walked back to my seat...a contented and satisfied man.

Tanie
THE PRESENT

Confused, I picked up the book—its jacket peeling, the cover old. I turned to the first page and then it hit me stronger than the lightning on a stormy day—an anchor on the seashore, an intuition to a disaster.

The page read:

This book belongs to Ishita Palathingal
who is giving it to Aaryan Gill,
and he wants Tanie to turn to page 33.

The plane was losing height, descending, taking me closer to Sumer. My ears hurt, my heart ached—ear pressure and heart pressure.

I quickly turned to page 33. There in the grip of the book rested a very familiar crumpled piece of paper—it was SUMER'S note! My hand went in my pocket in reflex to find everything but the note. How did Aaryan get my note? How? In mind-boggling confusion, I opened the note only to find inside another folded piece of paper with Air India's letterhead. I straightened its creases and began reading the folded piece of paper:

Her first dream, her first friend,
his company where she didn't need to pretend.
To her, there wasn't anything more appealing
and not very later, this gave to a much stronger feeling.
But oh girl! The two are poles apart.
Friendship is a responsibility, love a commitment,
all you've done is read Erich Segal and Margaret Mitchell,
but the reality, sadly, none of these tell.
She longed for his magical touch, his one look.
'Best friends' on the face, secretly she yearned for more that,
the hand she shook.
Wait oh, lass!
Let your heart not rule your brain,
let his words not drive you insane.
For him, you are just a comrade,
For him, love is a trade.

Stop oh damsel!
Do you even realize what path you are treading?
In silence, secret chains of admiration you are threading in
his happiness, you find solace.
His dream is your dream, chase.

Think my dear, you didnt stop when it was needed,
to your emotions, his heart never heeded.
You held his hand, while he searched for the one he wanted
to embrace.
His friendship to you is enough, it is God's holy grace.
Yet he hurt you, crumpled you, left you to die.
'We will always be together,' time and again he mouthed
the lie
and then he left her...
Numb she sits, drying her wet eyes
to escape his hauntings, in vain she tries.
Yet he remains unknown of what you feel,
his love, your broken heart still loves to conceal.

—Boza Korbi

Tanie, you dropped Sumer's note when you were paying for the coffee and I found it. Destiny or was this meant to be such, I really don't know but something in me made me go talk to you when I saw you sitting back there in the boarding lounge, the book in hand. You must have stopped for a second and wondered why was I sharing my story with you? Honestly I myself don't have an answer to this...just like we both collectively don't have an answer to how our life stories turned out to be so strangely familiar. It's not déjà vu; it's something much more stronger, much more eternal. I know I sound high but then you can blame it on the height of the plane (don't mind my joke). My handwriting may seem untidy to you, but it's the moving plane effect.

Now you must be wondering about the poem. Yes, it's Boza's poem. After reaching Singapore, I received an email from Karan. He had found this poem on Boza's laptop when she had left it with him before going out with her local guardians for a night's stay.

I received another email from Karan that evening. Boza was in hospital...her guardian's car had landed in a head-on collision with a truck. She was critical and here I was helpless... in Singapore, hating the seven days I had wished for so long now. I miss Boza; I miss the girl who would go to any extent for my happiness. I don't know if I love her or not, but yes, there is a very strong feeling—a feeling which is deeper than what I felt for Ishita, then or now. Perhaps it is right when people argue that it is very difficult for a guy and a girl to be just friends because at the end of the day, a bond is formed—a bond so secure, a bond which makes us so habitual to each other, a bond which makes us so...damn, I can't even explain to you what I feel! All I know is that Boza is still critical.

Tanie, I've once made the mistake of losing the person who cared for me more than myself...it's your choice now.

All the best for your life and do pray for Boza.

Touch down; the plane's wheels kissed the ground and tears automatically spilled from my eyes. I felt numb in every fucking part of me. The plane started to retard its pace, now moving slowly on the runway. The paper fell from my hand and there I was left with Sumer's note staring at me.

Sumer's note

Dear Tanie,

Hi! How are you? Okay listen, I am not really good at all this. I mean tearing pages neatly, or writing, or even getting senti about things and stuff but one thing Mom says and I believe is that, I am good at apologizing.

I am sorry Tanie if I hurt you that day. The last three months have been the loneliest of my life. First Liaka and then you...I was left all alone but I'm not complaining. I've been hearing from Mom how fab your pre-Boards and Boards went and I'm sure you'll nail the MUN in Singapore too. I met Megha the other day in the market and she told me that Rehaan apologized to you publicly. Honestly, I don't know myself what did Makrant bhaiya say or do to him...so Tanie, I just wanted to wish you all the best for your journey.

Just one last question—are we friends again? Please, can I pick you up from the road again or dance, wearing my boxers? If that's all it takes for you and me to become 'we' again. I miss you, I really do. Okay, I am running short of words and the pen is also exhausting its ink (Uday's pen, you see). So please, I will be waiting for your answer once you come back—just one answer and I swear I won't ever trouble you again.

And I'm sorry if this hurts you, but I LOVE YOU... and I can't help it.

The plane screeched to a halt and my heartbeat stopped. The world almost stopped. Everybody around me started to get up, gather their belongings, retrieve their handbags and move on. Everything else, but this!

My legs didn't react to the cerebral signals. My senses, my power to react—all failed; complete blackout.

'Ma'am, is everything alright,' an airhostess asked, walking up to me.

'Yes,' I said startled and looked around. The plane was almost empty...so was the seat Aaryan had occupied. Destiny is the answer to all questions or the biggest question to all answers!

'Ma'am, should I call for a doctor?' the airhostess asked me politely.

'No...no, no, I am fine,' I breathed deeply and bent down, picked up the piece of paper and folded it carefully. I was fine; in fact, I had never felt so sure of myself and my heart. I had an answer...I had a best friend again.

Acknowledgements

Thanking people is more difficult than eating ten Zinger burgers at KFC, at one go. Yet what cannot be overlooked is that, most of the time it's 'free' and surprisingly, it guarantees returns—royalty—yes, that's the word! So its time I stop proving why I am a good Commerce student and get down to business (pun intended).

Mom & Dad—behind my glories are your supportive hands, and behind my shortcomings are the times when your advice I did not care to understand.

Randeep Chachu & Priyanka Chachi—for cementing my belief in the word 'family'. I know I don't often say this but I really admire you.

Winkle & Twinkle—I think it's time I let the world and you both know that I consider myself to be the luckiest brother alive.

Family & Friends—(from Chandigarh to California)—all my *dost* and mostly the *saheliyan*, who let me (unwillingly) get my book in every conversation in the last few months. Thank you for being there in my life and, of course, the bookshops (now/in the near future) where my book is being/will be sold.

Just Friends could have not been possible without certain friends, who spread the fragrance of friendship in my life—

especially at the times it had started to stink.

Bani—Four years and we are still best friends—four years of happiness, pain, *pangas*, late-night group convos, after-tuition food overdrives—four years of a life lived and loved for (sometimes against) each other.

Chitvan—My only literate and educated friend (a lethal combo!). One of the very few who shared my vision and helped me realize it since its very inception.

Thank you Rupa Publications and your editorial, marketing and sales teams for their constant support and understanding.

All the MUNs I have participated in. Nupur, I found you there. Mashaal, my first reader and luckily a very good friend.

All the friends on Facebook, I have bugged repeatedly by sending sample chapters all the time! My short stint at Selaqui (Dehradun)…the writing bug bit me there, and Manisha Ma'am, you are responsible for that.

St. John's High School, Chandigarh—My *Alma Mater*. Here, I was taught not only to read but to understand, not only to write but to express. Thank you THE CRUCIBLE, thank you to all my English teachers: Z'nobia Ma'am, Priya Das Ma'am, Bhardwaj Ma'am, Pandarvani Ma'am and Rita Ma'am (the factual tests surely helped!).

Preeti Ma'am, Kadambni Ma'am (librarians)—All those official bunks and relaxation on over shooting the due date, almost every time… See, what it has led to!

Kavita Das Ma'am—You will always be the Principal with a difference. Thank you for teaching me values which go beyond texts.

Bhavan Vidyalaya, Panchkula—It is truly here that I got to spread my wings and soar to new heighs. Poonam Ma'am, English is the only class I don't deliberately bunk. Urvashi

Ma'am, you are the best.

Shashi Banerjee Ma'am—Your personality and aura as a Principal has always left me awestruck. Thank you, for letting me stay in the school despite my 'controversial' attendance record.

The British Library, Chandigarh—You gave me the setting and the atmosphere to finish writing my book. Not to forget the friends I made during my one-month stint there.

Thank YOU readers...for sparing your (not so) precious time and thinking of buying this book, for whatever ulterior motive.

AND, IN THE END, I want to mention the angel (who can't be named as yet), who actually taught me what *love* and *friendship* is all about...